'We need to make a move now if we're going to pull this off.' He stood, swung round alongside her. Cupped her face with his hands. 'Trust me. I won't hurt you. I'll take care of you.'

She almost choked. They were words that should belong in a real marriage proposal. Words that would have her melting and sobbing a grateful 'yes'. But this was a business marriage and a business deal.

'I'll do it,' she said.

He smiled. His eyes crinkled and flashed. He dipped his lips and planted a soft, warm kiss on her mouth.

'Good.'

He kissed her again. Just for a moment. Full on her lips. And her feral cat desire for him sprang up, startling her. What did *that* add to the mix of this fake marriage? Trouble…

Dear Reader

How many times have you had a goal in mind, an end point, a glittering prize that seems to be almost within reach? And then, when your fingers finally close around it, you realise it wasn't what you wanted or, more importantly, what you needed after all.

Well, this is what happens to Dubai's hottest bachelor—Danny Ryan. Even the planets align for Danny, because all hell is let loose when they don't, but when a meteor hits his path in the shape of the lovely Georgia he learns that 'It's my way or the highway' isn't the only rule in town.

At the start of this book, when Georgia walks into a seven-star hotel, I wondered how on earth she would heal his tortured soul. She seems to have it all: beauty, wit, intelligence and strength. Still not enough for an inferno like Danny... But by the end of the book, when she turns out to be a composite of all the most dedicated educators I've ever met, I knew he was toast. Above all of her qualities it's her selfless compassion that shines most brightly. And when you have that as much as she does the *only* fitting prize is Danny Ryan.

I loved these characters! I hope you do too.

With my warmest wishes

Bella

THE SCANDAL BEHIND THE WEDDING

BY
BELLA FRANCES

MILLS &
BOON

Published in Great Britain 2015
by Mills & Boon, an imprint of Harlequin (UK) Limited,
Eton House, 18-24 Paradise Road, Richmond, Surrey, TW9 1SR

© 2015 Bella Frances

ISBN: 978-0-263-24947-7

Harlequin (UK) Limited's policy is to use papers that are natural, renewable and recyclable products and made from wood grown in sustainable forests. The logging and manufacturing processes conform to the legal environmental regulations of the country of origin.

Printed and bound in Spain
by CPI, Barcelona

Unable to sit still without reading, **Bella Frances** first found romantic fiction at the age of twelve, in between deadly dull knitting patterns and recipes in the pages of her grandmother's magazines. An obsession was born! But it wasn't until one long, hot summer, after completing her first degree in English Literature, that she fell upon the legends that are Mills & Boon® books. She has occasionally lifted her head out of them since to do a range of jobs, including barmaid, financial adviser and teacher, as well as to practise (but never perfect) the art of motherhood to two (almost grown-up) cherubs.

Her eclectic collection of wonderful friends have provided more than their fair share of inspiration for heroes, heroines and glamorous locations, and it was while waiting to board a flight home after a particularly lively holiday that the characters for her first competition success in *So You Think You Can Write* were born.

Bella lives a very energetic life in the UK, but tries desperately to travel for pleasure at least once a month—strictly in the interests of research!

Catch up with her on her website at www.bellafrances.co.uk

Another Modern Tempted™ title by Bella Frances:

DRESSED TO THRILL

This and other titles by Bella Frances are available in eBook format from www.millsandboon.co.uk

To Team O
(the 'ahead of the game' years)

CHAPTER ONE

HEART THUDDING THUNDERCLAP-LOUD in her ears, Georgia Blue climbed out of her sand-strewn sedan and tossed the keys to the valet parker. In her best…okay, *only* vintage Alaïa dress, she looked as if she could actually *afford* to be a resident here. Crazy how easy it was to pull on a piece of old Lycra, stuff heat-stroked tootsies into razor-sharp slingbacks and strut your way into paradise.

She cut a path through the lobby of the seven-star Al-Jafar, the swish and sway of guests blending into a blur of colour and monochrome. Between the dots of majestic palms and bejewelled pillars the spectacular central fountain bubbled liquid wealth, and in between the couture, the businesswear and the downright casual, black *abayas* and white *kanduras* reminded her that, ruby slingbacks aside, she wasn't in east London any more. Or even anywhere near it.

She passed by the wide, welcoming lounge and straight to the elevators. Times she had sipped iced water with Nick on those sofas flashed through her mind—gorgeous days. When there had still been a chance that old Alaïa might one day make friends with new Alaïa. When the half-carat diamond on her finger had flashed happily, sure that a band of gold would one day join it. Not like now, when her ring was the definition of solitaire. Tucked away with her pride in its little velvet box. Now the best downtime could offer was a beach club Happy Hour in between the two jobs that kept money flowing back home.

And this. This 'party'. This *will-I-won't-I?*, *what-have-I-got-to-lose?* singles party that her roommate Kirsty had told her about. While the rest of her buddies were all packing their overnight bags to head out of town for a girlie weekend what else was she going to do? Trail social media sites and post fake comments about the awesome time she was having?

No. It was well past time she got a grip on the gloom and took some control back. A singles party was just what she needed. So what if she was dreading it? Could it be *that* bad?

She poked a seen-much-better-days manicured fingernail to call the elevator. Another luxury that would have to go. Brass doors opened. Smoky mirrors reflected the net result of putting make-up on in a car, on a half-built road, in the middle of a sandstorm, with five minutes to spare. She was Cleopatra-dramatic with the eyes, and the wonky lip-liner round her mouth made it look much more trout than pout.

Her confidence was already borderline neurotic even without a make-up malfunction—enough to tip her over the edge and into the car back home and a hot date with the television. Yes, that sounded perfect.

She paused, swivelled round to leave. A figure appeared behind her, blocking the light and her path back out. Tall, dark and sharp in executive clothes. Super-hot. And even through the haze of her mascara-caked eyelashes he looked kettlebell-fit. She caught his eye before she got a chance to spin round and hide her face between the twin curtains of dark red hair that for once in her life was all soft waves instead of ponytail-sensible. If Babs could see her now she'd never believe it—her tomboy baby sister looking like a drag queen with stage fright.

Georgia stood in the corner, eyes swept down, staring at his shoes. They had to be handmade. And Italian. They stepped inside and turned, with their owner, to face first her and then the control panel in the corner. Noise came next. Voices…male. Laughing and easy and fun. They piled right in through her line of vision. She swept her eyes up past them. The ceiling was *so* much more interesting.

Young rich men were ten a penny in this town—and this lot brought a noise and a scent that bellowed the fact that they'd been on a liquid-only brunch.

A slight hush as they piled inside and then the doors closed, pushing them closer. They'd noticed her. Over here everybody noticed her—even in her default bare-faced-and-boring look. Paper-pale skin and long auburn hair were not the easiest things to keep under wraps— but add to that an explosion in a make-up factory and a no-imagination-needed dress and she guaranteed herself an audience of gaping man cubs.

'Excuse me, miss?'

Dark, deep and disquieting, Italian-Shoes-Man's tones cut through the crush and jolted her eyes back down.

'Which floor?'

She flashed a glance at the array of illuminated golden circles. At a Dubai-bronzed masculine hand hovering, waiting for her reply.

'Which floor?' he repeated patiently.

His accent was hard to place—a native English-speaker, though the soft burr made her think of rugged coastlines and rolling fields. Cosy pubs and pints of stout. Comfort. But the man himself, when she trailed her eyes from outstretched hand to broad shoulder and proud jaw, was clean-line city.

In the crush of boozy testosterone he stood apart. Taller, fiercer. Power oozed like strong cologne and she scented it, unwillingly. Powerful men were hard work. They made demands and expected returns. Their egos took more maintenance than her manicure. She dealt with them enough at work to know they were exactly the kind of men to stay well away from.

And he had those thick, sharp, gull wing brows going on.

She rolled her eyes. There was something deeply un-attractive about a man with better eyebrows than you. Nick was like that. But Nick was a jerk—who admit-tedly waxed, plucked and tinted *his* eyebrows. Beyond vain. In love with himself and the idea of love. Shallow as that fountain and false as the Dubai Mall ski-slopes. Wow, she'd been such a fool.

'Miss?' The still patient tones jolted her back.

'Fifty-ninth, thank you,' she said, seeing the circle al-ready illuminated.

Yes, she'd been even more gullible than usual when she'd met Nick. But this guy, even though he was smooth and sleek, actually looked hard and more than a little bit tough—a force. Elemental and real. As if he had stubble because he hadn't had a chance to shave—not because the men's magazines were showcasing stubble this sea-son. As if he'd picked up the bump on the side of his nose on a rugby field or in a barroom brawl. *As if he'd know exactly how to use those lips.*

And the gull wings, now that she saw more closely, were really just thick, naturally well-shaped brows to set off his freakishly perfect blue eyes.

The elevator zoomed, stilled, and then the doors eased

open just a few floors higher. There was barely space inside for a blast of cheap perfume but a middle-aged couple thought they'd give it a go. The guys shifted and pressed closer to her. In her heels she was nose to nose with the smallest of them, and they were all pretty tall. She could sense them exchanging looks, then heard a stifled snigger. Whatever. They were totally *not* getting to her and her manufactured composure.

She was late. She was heading into the unknown. But she was determined to stop being a victim. And she was going to project cool and calm—starting now.

The elevator whooshed and paused again, to deposit the couple, but the guy closest didn't give back her personal space. Instead he turned round and winked. Really. *Winked*. She drew her eyes from him and stared straight ahead.

'Hey, gorgeous, how about it?'

Georgia opened her mouth to flip out her standard, *You couldn't afford me*. The line she served up with the pints and shots she passed across the bar of The Tavern—London pub and home to her and Babs since forever. But that would just get her into a conversation, and they were too young, too cocksure and too much the worse for their liquid brunch for her to go anywhere near them.

No, much better if she focussed on chatting to men who were maybe a bit older tonight, a bit quieter, a bit more homely than off-the-charts handsome—maybe a man she could…*trust*?

After all since Nick had gone, taking with him the stuffing he'd knocked out of her, the last thing she needed was to get all bent out of shape over another hot young dude. Or—worse still—someone like the power furnace in the corner. The one who was burning up the air in this elevator with no more than his presence. A guy like that was an incendiary device. And she wanted a slow burn, not spontaneous combustion. *Didn't she?*

She could feel the thudding starting in her ears again as the number fifty-nine remained illuminated. She could feel the tension rise in the tiny cramped space as the guys re-started their testosterone-fuelled rumbling. She could feel Italian-Shoe-Man watching her closely. And she felt her eyes slide to his as she stared right back.

Georgia had to have laid eyes on hundreds and hundreds of men and boys in her twenty-six years of serving drinks, coaching football and teaching pre-schoolers. But the eyes of this man lasered right through her and jolted her harder than if the elevator had just crashed. She felt compelled to stare. She felt as if he could see right inside her. And right here, right now, anyone staring into her mess of homesick, heartsick and sick-to-her-stomach broke, was staring into something she'd much rather keep cloaked.

He didn't flinch or shift his eyes. They were just— *there*. Watching…absorbing. But she was smart enough to know that, looking the way he did, he had to have a first-class degree in flirting. No way she could let herself get caught up in something as dangerous as flirting right back. Not when she was looking for a quiet, fade-into-the-background kind of guy. Someone who would cosset her, look after her and smooth her ruffled feathers. Someone who wouldn't ask her and every other girl within a ten-thousand-mile radius to marry him. Even though *this* guy looked as if marriage was the last thing on his mind…

He didn't smile, and when the doors suddenly started to close she was jolted into realising that he was probably just intrigued by how one person could wear so much make-up and not melt under the weight. And her dress, when she glanced down at it, was doing just what Alaïa had intended—flattering and flaunting.

His boozy friend broke the silence.

'Come on—let's get to the party. I need to get my hands on some ass…'

'Tommy, mind your manners. There's a lady present.'

It was quietly said but everyone hushed instantly. His eyes never left hers and her skin scorched all the way from her hot pinched toes to her hair-laquered head. He looked serious—deadly serious—and she felt a sudden intense kick of adrenalin…or fear…or some other overwhelming feeling. *Trouble*. That was what it was.

Time to go.

She forced herself to move. Some of them pressed back to give her a little space and she manoeuvred her sharp shoes forward.

Taking a calming breath, she stepped out of the elevator and into a broad, long corridor gleaming with the light from a thousand chandeliers and reflecting miles of pale polished marble. A small gold sign showed two choices—five suites to the left and five suites to the right. She chose left. There was silence now, apart from the light click of her heels.

In a shower of golden light a balcony opened up on her right, overhanging the atrium drop to the outrageous fountain which flowed with unadulterated affluence. The corridor swept ahead, its smooth wall curling out of sight. She clicked round, the echoes following the curve. Finally there were two doors to the left. Equally imperious. She walked right up to one. Another small golden sign: Jumeirah Suite.

This was it.

She reached her hand forward and braced herself for an hour of air-kissing and a super-bright smile.

The door swung open.

Georgia stared blankly from the very large man in western clothes who had opened it to the scene within. Riches, opulence, glamour. People—men and beautiful women. Her feet continued their self-directed path and went right in.

The place was huge. Which was no surprise, really—seven-star hotels would have seven-star suites—with more riches per square inch than Aladdin's Cave. Still, even after six months in Dubai she was completely unprepared for what she saw.

Twin marble staircases descended with a swirl to a sunken lounge furnished with white leather sofas, over-dressed with gold and china-blue satin cushions. On the mezzanines at either side were more seating areas, one with a bar and one with diner-style booths—all pale blue studded leather and filmy white and gold drapes. The wall behind the staircases was made entirely of glass—easily sixty feet of it—and behind that sat the magnificent Persian Gulf, its blue hues melding with the lilacs and oranges of the early evening sun.

But she'd seen a sunset or ten, stepped out on more than her fair share of marble, and lounged on lots of butter-soft leather. So it wasn't the opulence that was immediately arresting. It was the rest of it that was so striking. Singles? *Couples.* Reclining on low white leather sofas, drinks in hand, and looking very, *very* relaxed. Even through the air-con there was a heady sense of hedonism. Strange for a singles' party—even here.

She looked around for other girls like her, but every girl was occupied—*very* occupied—with a man.

Georgia's eyes warred with her brain and her mouth with her feet to figure out which was going to take action first. A woman climbed one of the stairs towards her. Silky black hair and almond-black eyes. Red mouth and red one-shoulder silk dress cut to the thigh. It made her Alaïa feel more like a nun's habit.

'Hi—I'm not sure if I'm in the right place. I was told just to show up. This is a singles party, right?'

The stunning woman ignored her. Flicked her a derisory head-to-toe glance, arched the most perfect brow, quirked the most perfect lip and walked right on by. She paused at a bar area, trailed a scarlet nail down the cheek of a corpulent businessman. He placed his hand on her backside and squeezed. Georgia watched, transfixed, as the woman arched her back and allowed him to touch her breast.

She was not the type of woman who sang nursery rhymes to four-year-olds or who had bruises from junior football. These were not homespun girls looking for Mr Right. Oh, no. These women were sophisticated, sexy, and setting out their stalls.

Georgia looked around again for something—*any-thing*—to anchor herself to. But the whole scene was just plain weird. How could everyone be hooked up already? Okay, she'd never been to a singles party before, but she'd heard enough stories about speed-dating to figure that not *everyone* would be coupled up at…what?… seven-thirty p.m. In fact, when she looked a little closer, some couples were actually threes. *Uh-oh.*

She felt as if she was standing on the deck of a sinking ship and sharks were circling closer. If this was dipping her toe into the dating waters she'd keep herself on the warm, dry land of singlehood, thank you.

Yes, this was definitely a mistake. She'd go back to the complex. She'd have the place all to herself since everyone else would already be on a flight to Ras al Khaimah. She'd soak in the plunge pool. She'd watch TV and text

Kirsty to tell her that this was her worst *ever* piece of dating advice.

Maybe she would see if there were any more companies hiring junior coaches. She still had a couple of week nights free to pick up work, after all. The kids would give her a reason to smile, and any extra cash would be a bonus for Babs. Really—that was what she should be focussing everything on.

It was kind of the girls to suggest she start dating again, but even though she was well over Nick she was well short of the money she wanted to send Babs. Sixty thousand in legal fees and loans was going to take ages to pay—even in tax-free Dubai.

She turned around, ready to leave, more determined than ever to get out of this crazy party. The door opened again. Noise and lots of it—the boozy boys. A crack of command to silence them…dark, disquieting tones…and then cobalt eyes fastened straight onto hers.

She watched as they all piled in. His gang—because there was no doubt that he was the leader—all had their eyes on stilts, as if it was Christmas morning and the gifts were all for them. He stood at the door, letting them go, eyes only on her.

She stalled. She wavered. He waited. And watched. And then he took the decision right out of her hands and walked up to her. Not too fast, not too lazily, but sure and solid—no room for debate.

A slash of white suddenly lit his face, changing it from intense to exceptional as the brightness of his eyes was matched by the brilliance of his smile. He was breathtaking—it almost hurt her eyes to look at him. And to think she'd once thought Nick hot and handsome! This man aced every man-measuring yardstick. He was up close now, and she tipped her head back slightly to look at him.

He had that reassuring height that made her feel feminine. A chest broad enough to lay her head on and melt into. Strength and stature…looks and presence. If there were man trophies his shelves would be covered in them.

'Hi. Good to meet you…again.'

She watched stupidly as he lifted her puppet-like arm and brought her hand to his mouth. His lips were warm with an edge of soft stubble. She felt her eyes widen as he pressed them against her skin and struggled even more to keep up. He lowered her hand, pulled her a little closer and curved his lips into the sexiest smile she'd ever seen. The promise of long, slow and sensual loving was right there in the quirk of his lips. *Terrifying.*

'What's your name?'

'Georgia.' She breathed out her name and allowed him to keep her hand in his for a moment, still locked into that stare.

'Georgia. Beautiful name,' he said.

Was blue the colour of sin? She thought so—it was laced through his eyes.

'Danny Ryan.'

'Hi,' she said back, finding her voice and a bit of composure.

She shook the hand that he had wrapped in his own and wondered where on earth her default defence mechanisms were. This man was super-league in every sense. Meaning that her run-for-your-life hormones should be pumping, instead of her gooey-girl hormones.

Come on, get back in the game—bath, bed and beyond is where you're headed. Then a trawl for another job. The last thing you need is to get caught up in something like this with someone like him.

'It's nice to meet you, Danny. But I'm afraid I seem to have wound up at the wrong…' She looked around, wondering how you would actually describe this. 'I think I'm totally at the wrong party.'

He let her fingers slip away when she tugged her hand free, but held her with that presence, or force-field, or whatever it was.

'Well, that's a pity, because I was hoping to get the chance to properly apologise for what happened earlier. The boys have been working flat-out—they've had a couple of drinks and are being a bit loose with their tongues. I had a word with them—all of them—before we came in here. I hope you weren't offended. Apologies—they meant no harm.'

'Thanks, but since it wasn't you who offended me there's no need to apologise—and I am *really* in the wrong place. So…'

She looked around at his group who'd brought a whole new energy to the place. A place she really didn't feel very comfortable in—even with the hottest guy in the room so up close and personal. *Especially* with the hottest guy in the room so up close and personal.

'So. Yes. Thanks. Nice to meet you but I'm going to head off.'

He frowned slightly. Very slightly. As if he hadn't quite given her permission to leave. You had to laugh at these guys. Clearly not used to anyone doing anything other than fall into line. But the adrenalin had definitely kicked in now and she'd decided on flight not fight. She was *so* not going there. What would be the point? He would think that she was a lot more liberal than she was just by virtue of actually being in this crazy place. And even though she badly needed some attention, a little bit of salve for her bruised and battered ego, she'd prefer it was with someone who would settle her down rather than stir her up.

'Tommy.'

He didn't so much bark out the name as growl it. And instantly the pain in the neck from the elevator appeared before her. His nose was sunburned and his eyes were slightly glazed. But he was lapdog-ready where his boss was concerned and he issued an instant apology.

'Really sorry for what I said…and did…in the lift.'

'Forget it,' she said, looking away, looking for a clear path out.

But things were beginning to happen. Girls were coming forward, smiling and flirting. Heading right for the guys like homing devices. They were of all races. And all beautiful. Tall, cool, blonde. Hot Latino. Dusky, dramatic, dark. Pouty, elegant, ebony. And, yes, Celtic and pale. A smorgasbord. Were they all single? Really? Or had she arrived at a very different type of party?

Tommy didn't hang around—he went straight back to the boys, swung his arms round two stunning girls and moved off, laughing as if this was the best Christmas Day *ever*.

She looked at Danny Ryan. Oh, no. He must think she was as easy as them. And—worse—he must be looking for that kind of girl. No way a guy like him was single by choice. None. Not a chance. The sands were still shifting. The waters were deep. And deadly. Time to swim for the shore.

'I've got to go.' She grabbed her bag tightly to her side, made to leave. Didn't want to be there a moment longer.

'Wait,' he said, reaching out for her hand. 'Why don't you hang around a bit?'

'I'm sorry,' she said. 'That's not going to happen. This is *not* my kind of party.'

He looked around, frowned. 'Yeah, I know what you mean. It's not at all what I was expecting either.'

He focussed his piercing stare back on her. As if it would compel her to stay.

'Why don't we find somewhere a bit more—civilised?'

She tried to look away from those eyes—she really did. But they took some amount of staring—so many blues…not a trace of cloudy grey or mossy green…just blue and black and deep. You could easily lose hours of your life staring into eyes like those—just looking for a flaw. But she didn't want to waste any more of her life. She wanted to get her life back. Back on track. Back to earning as much as she possibly could, so that she could start to clear some of Babs's debts and then finally get on a plane and the longed-for flight home.

'Thanks, but I think I'll head home. I'm not really in the mood now.'

He swung another glance around, frowned a little more. Seemed to check out what his boys were getting up to.

She did the same and saw that they were getting past first base and straight to third without so much as a casual introduction. This wasn't a singles party. This was a brothel!

'Give me a minute—I need to check in with my boys. They don't know what we've wandered into. Then we'll go somewhere else to fix your mood.'

He pinned her in place with a confident nod and then called a couple of his guys over to chat. She could go—she *should* go. Nausea was beginning to form in her throat. She knew this kind of party went on—she wasn't stupid. But she'd never been up close and personal to it. She'd never seen with her own eyes—girls who could be her or her friends—girls dressed for a club night. But the only club they were going to was one that paid their wages.

She didn't want to judge, but if this was what she thought it was she really didn't belong here. And she certainly didn't want to be hooking up with any guy—no matter how gorgeous—at a place like this.

He was still rounding up his team—some of whom looked less than impressed that he was calling time on their fun. Some of the girls stared over at her. If looks could kill...

Definitely time to go. She pulled the strap of her bag tighter, squared her shoulders and headed to the door.

Suddenly there was a noise and the crowd of girls and guys in front of her melted away. She looked up to see the cause of the commotion. Uniformed men. Police. Oh, no—could this get any worse?

Danny Ryan appeared at her side. Grabbed her hand.

'What's happening? Why are the police here?'

'Only one reason I can think of. And it's not making me feel reassured. Come on.'

He sounded grim. Formidable. And something in her urged her to lean into the strength that he was channelling.

He moved fast towards the stairs. Her slingbacks slipped and clicked, keeping up with his lengthy strides.

'I could be wrong, but I'd guess this is an unlicensed party and someone has forgotten to pay off the right person. That would explain why there's more than fizz and canapés on offer.'

'What? What do you mean? I *knew* there was something weird going on! I was told this was a singles party—I'm a kindergarten teacher. I can't afford to get caught up in anything!'

'None of us can, Georgia. None of us can.'

They landed at the bottom of the long twist of marble and stepped out onto the wide wraparound terrace—complete with plunge pool—stuck on the side of the building, hundreds of feet in the air. Bodies lazed and lounged, still oblivious of the raid upstairs. Bronzed limbs in every conceivable pose.

She looked away. Didn't want to see any more of what was clearly happening all around her. The unfurling commotion was rapidly turning into a living nightmare. Panic was setting in. She had commitments. She had Babs—her life-saver, who had sacrificed everything to bring her up, to give her a good home and was relying on her and her tax-free salary just to make ends meet. She couldn't possibly jeopardise that!

'But you don't understand—I *can't* get into trouble here. I could lose my job. I could get arrested.'

'I've no intention of letting anyone get arrested. Or lose their job.' He sounded half distracted. 'Here—this way. I've got the perfect place to wait it out.'

They moved now on plush velvet carpet. Her heels sank and she stumbled a little, trying to keep up. He turned, shot her an intense steadying look, and then scooped her close to his side. She heard the rumble of the commotion now above them.

'What about your team?'

'I've told them what to do and say if they get into trouble. They'll be fine as long as they remember.' He paused for another second, gave her another calming look. 'You'll be fine too.'

She could only hope so. She'd been warned when she'd arrived in Dubai—they all had—not to get into any trouble. Especially with the police. She worked for an international school with hugely high standards and any fun was to be had within strict boundaries.

But who would believe she was innocent? That she had come to this party thinking she might find a date?

She looked just like those girls—with a tight dress and too much make-up. If she got taken to the police station she'd have to tell them where she lived. Then they'd know she worked at the international school. And that would be it. She'd be sent home in disgrace. Or worse. Jailed.

They were out in the hallway again. Same golden light, same bubbling fountain. But one floor down.

A solid door—mother-of-pearl. He slid a key and pulled it open. A private elevator, all glass and brass.

'In here.'

She wavered. For a moment it felt as if she was on the cusp of the hugest decision of her life.

'Is this safe? Is it going to be all right?'

He squeezed her hand. 'Look, you'll be fine. I know enough people here to get things sorted. I think we'll be fine up here—away from the main action—until things settle.'

He cocked one eyebrow. "Okay?"

She nodded and followed him—decision made.

Inside, with the doors closed, up it zoomed, flying up the outer edge of the building. They had to be at the very top now—in a penthouse.

Finally the doors opened and, yes, sure enough…

Wow! This was a Honeymoon, Presidential, Penthouse—and then some. An entire picture wall of glass to her right, the perfect array of furniture to lounge upon and view it from to her left—all overhung with a deep, high balcony and lit by enormous silk-shaded lamps. Glimpses of stairs leading to a rooftop terrace, of other rooms—opulent, magnificent, utterly unparalleled. A grand piano here, a twenty-seat table there. Art on the walls that she definitely recognised. She felt as if even the air was weightier, worthier.

He led her inside.

'Is this okay while we wait?' He moved in through the space, perfectly at home.

She trailed behind him, wary of this luxury, unease twisting at her gut. She was not the type of girl who ever got into trouble. Not at school. Not at college. Not at home. Never. She knew right from wrong. And the only wrong thing she'd ever done was to believe in her fairytale engagement.

'Hey. It's all right.' Danny stopped. Walked back to face her. Looked right at her and ran his hands up and down her arms.

She gazed up at him, desperately trying to keep it together. 'I can't afford to get into trouble. I need my job. It's all I have.'

He nodded and she felt strangely reassured. She had no reason to trust him, but her instincts told her she was better off in this majestic wonderland with him than back at that party arguing her point alone. And it wasn't only the fact that he radiated composure. There was no denying the unmistakable sensual tension he was building as he soothed and stroked her arms.

His eyes dropped to her mouth. She licked her lips.

But he shook his head, sucked in a breath through his teeth and led her to the low-seated area. 'Why don't you sit here? I'm going to make a couple of calls.'

His voice was low, lilting and calming. But his energy was tense. And she felt it. *Oh, yes.*

He stood beside her as she sat down warily, felt firm stuffed silk cushions against her back. From a tiny Aladdin's lamp on the table at her side a drift of scented oil wound around her, languorous and loose. Opposite, ivory orchids in golden pots along the window wall sat like daubs of paint on a canvas of blue, marred only by the gleam and thrust of yet another iconic superstructure rearing up out of the Gulf.

He let go of her hand but trailed his touch up her arm and gently under her chin. She tilted her head to look at him. He locked that gaze on her again. So strong. Unyielding.

He shook his head, as if he couldn't quite believe what he was doing or why. Touched a finger to her lips, nodded slightly, and then turned. Took a pace away and swiped out his phone.

'Sarwar? Hey. It's Danny. Look, I need a favour...'

CHAPTER TWO

RISK. AND THE management thereof. Normally one of his strong suits. Normally something he took a lot of pride in being very, *very* good at. The kind of deals he made required it. And although he'd had all of five minutes' formal training—in other words read some stuff on the net—he'd become so well respected for the completely researched, planned and executed-within-a-hair's-breadth decisions he made that his view was sought on projects well outside his own corporate boundaries.

So what on earth was he doing, tucked in the penthouse of the Al-Jafar, having bailed out of a highly dodgy party with an utterly gorgeous redhead who had caused chaos since he'd first slapped eyes on her?

Just getting out of her car she had been impressive. She probably didn't even know that one guy had kerbed his coupé in the parking bay at the entrance as he watched her swing into the hotel. And that another guy had been slapped out of his daydream by his wife as he'd stared open-mouthed at her walking through the lobby. Danny had truly never seen a woman walk with such an unconscious sense of her own sexual allure.

And Tommy in the lift… If it hadn't been so crass it would have been funny. It was as if the guy had been in a trance. His eyes had roamed all over the lovely Georgia, standing right there, her perfect breasts outlined in easily the sexiest piece of clothing he had ever seen. Okay, it was up to her neck and down to her knees—Dubai-appropriate—but nothing short of a tent could cover a body like *that*.

Tommy hadn't even known he'd touched her—or so he'd said when he'd given him 'the talk' back in the lift. This was not a town where you stepped out of line in public. You just couldn't risk it. Even when the eye candy was as sweet as their little lift companion. Even *he'd* had to fight to keep his eyes respectfully at eye rather than chest level.

But now they had a situation to deal with. And one he'd never imagined when he'd accepted the invitation to come here. He'd thought his views on this kind of thing were well enough known for his business partners to leave out sweeteners like these. Still, this one had been set up by a new guy in town who probably assumed all red-blooded males liked to pay their way. Not him. No way. Never had and never would.

But how the lovely Georgia had ended up there was another thing. She'd looked shocked when they'd arrived. Standing in the middle of all that madness like Joan of Arc. A particularly sexy Joan of Arc, but definitely in a different class from the girls who were offering themselves for rent. She had an air about her…dignity. Now, even with cops prowling all over the place and the fall-out that was highly likely, she looked poised as a princess sitting on that sofa.

But he would find out more about her later—he had to focus on damage limitation right now. He clicked off the phone. Sarwar would smooth things. As the General Commander of Police he usually could. He was a handy ally to have—that was for sure. His only other concern was the press—the Dubai snappers were getting a bit invasive and he really didn't want any photos flying over satellites to his mother's news feed. He'd spent ten solid years here, building up his reputation, making her proud of him again—the last thing he wanted was for her to have any doubts at all.

After all, he'd built half of this town. Had made getting on here a personal challenge. His engineering skills had got him so far. But his corporate head had netted him contract upon contract and ally upon ally. There weren't a lot of Westerners who held as much sway as he did. He had some very close friends. Emirati friends. And he'd be damned if he was going to let anything shake his well-crafted reputation now.

He looked over to where Georgia was still sitting on the edge of the sofa, worry painted all over her beautiful face. She was right to be concerned about this. If she was as genuine as he thought she was then she could afford the reputational damage even less than he.

He walked back towards her and she stood up. Her fists were clenched in tight little twists.

'I checked in with a friend. It's going to be okay. We just need to sit it out for a while.'

'Who's your friend? How does he know what's going on?'

'Just a contact. But don't worry—a contact with a lot of influence. So, as I say, his advice is to wait it out while they sweep the place. Seems they're taking a bit of a firmer line with that type of party. Someone's decided to stop turning a blind eye.'

'Shame he didn't tell you that before you came.' It was sharply said.

'It is, yes—but since I never normally attend these sorts of events he wouldn't have known to warn me.'

Seemed he had already been judged and sentenced. Normally he wouldn't give a damn about anyone's opinion of him—other than his folks back home, of course—but for some reason he really wanted to underline the point with her that paying for sex was not his thing.

'I like to treat my boys when they've worked hard—and I got an invite to this party from a business contact. I wouldn't have gone if I'd known what was going on.'

She hesitated. Definitely still wary and more than a little bit cautious. Why did he feel the need to soothe her? But he did. Even with her snippy little tones he wanted to enfold her in his arms and smooth away her worries.

He took another step towards her. 'I'm glad I did, though, because our paths might not have crossed otherwise.'

She swallowed. His eye fell to the length of her neck, the sheen of her pale skin, the rise of her chest as she breathed. She looked from him to the door, listening. But this was the ultra-luxury penthouse, his home from home, and they were far enough away from the main action that no sounds would penetrate. Sarwar had said all the girls were going to be taken in. But he doubted that they would all go quietly. Better to be well away from *that* particular action.

'How long do you think we'll need to wait?'

'We can leave any time you like. I guarantee you'll not get into any difficulties with the police. I just think it politic not to catch the eye of the media or flaunt the position and the influence I have—so, unless you've got something more pressing to do, why don't we enjoy the view? Salvage what we can out of our Friday night?'

He trailed his gaze over her again. Heavy-lidded dark green eyes, clear and vital. Perfect smooth skin with a shimmer of freckles through the make-up. Wide, full mouth…slightly open. He loved her lips. Sensual lips. He couldn't take his eyes off how plump they looked—wondered how rich and sweet they'd taste. And that thick, soft dark red hair that framed her perfect face… Not to mention the rest of her. She was a beauty. A sensual, beautiful woman.

'How about a drink? What do you say, Georgia?'

He smiled at her—couldn't help it. She wore her thoughts on her face, unfiltered. She liked him. But she was still too wary to relax. He'd give her a little time, a little encouragement. It would be worth it. It wasn't every day that a girl like this fell into his path, albeit unwillingly. For once he might chase. It had been so, *so* long since he had.

He went over to the bar.

'Wine? Cocktail? I can do you a mean martini.'

She sat rooted to the couch and only turned her head to watch him. Again that princess posture. 'A glass of white wine would be fine. Thanks.'

He lifted two bottles from the chiller. Compared them. Chose a fruity dry Italian that had a light effervescence over a mellow Australian. It would be good to lift her spirits a little. Get rid of some of her tension.

He twisted, poured and extended a glass towards her. Finally she moved—pushing herself up off the low couch and meeting him in the middle of the giant glass wall. He tipped his glass against hers, tried to give her a reassuring smile. Her eyes roamed over his face. Landed on his mouth. Lingered there. So she liked what she saw. *Good.*

'You want to go up onto the roof terrace? See if we can hear the oil flow?'

She smiled. Just a little.

'I'm okay in here, thanks. Humidity is not my hair's

best friend. Anyway, I'm sure your conversation will flow better than any oil.'

'Yeah, well, hopefully we'll be out of here before it runs out. Or before Dubai runs out of crazy ideas to net every last tourist on the planet. I'd hate to miss anything.' He nodded back to the seating area. 'Are you all right there? Look safe enough for your hair?'

A tiny smile. 'Deal.'

She nudged her glass against his. She was definitely beginning to warm up. He walked behind her to the sofa, noting her sky-high shoulders settle down a little.

'Will we start with the obligatory ex-pat back story?'

He eased himself down beside her, put his glass down, stretched out his arms. He'd keep alcohol off the menu until he was off the premises and had an apology in his back pocket for being given that party invitation. He still couldn't believe he'd been caught up in something like this. He practically had the keys to this city—and thank God the pass to this penthouse, his weekend lair. Because now—when his deal with the Sheikh was at a critical stage—he would allow no one and nothing to get in his way.

He waited until she'd settled herself. Great posture. Great legs. She sipped her wine and watched him.

'Okay. I'll go first. My name's Daniel Leo Ryan. I'm thirty-four years old. I have one younger sister, Frankie. And one older brother, Mark. Italian mother, Irish father, regulation number of aunts and uncles. We hail from County Meath, outside Dublin, Ireland. The family breeds horses. I make buildings.'

That was enough to be going on with. The less savoury details could come later—or not at all.

'So do you ride? Or race?'

'I was put on a horse before I could walk. We all

were. It's non-negotiable in our family. Riding, grooming, mucking out. Very little time left for anything else. My brother is involved in the family business. Parents too. Frankie does her own thing—like me.' Though he was never sure what that was from one month to the next. 'And you, Georgia? You're definitely English. No mistaking that. London?'

She smiled at him. Finally. Properly. And it was glorious. A big toothy grin and it suited her.

'Yes. East End. Cockney. Born and raised in a pub called The Tavern. My full name is Georgia Anne Blue. I'm twenty-six. My mum passed away not long after I was born and my sister Babs—Barbara, but no one calls her that—she's eighteen years older than me—well, she brought me up. Rented out the pub until she was old enough to take it on herself. Put her whole life on hold for me. Never even had a proper boyfriend until I went to college.'

He nodded. That was a family dynamic he couldn't begin to imagine. There would be no place for sibling rivalry there—no competition, no fierce jealousy. No judging, comparing, winning. Just a tiny family, pulling together.

'What a huge sacrifice. You must be very close?'

She nodded, toyed with her glass a little.

'Totally. I owe her everything. She runs that pub like a dream, but there was no way she was going to allow *me* to settle for that. I was going to college—end of story.'

He nodded—could sympathise with that. Engineering was not exactly a skill that sat well with breeding thoroughbreds. Law, accountancy, business admin—those were the preferred courses, the ones to which his siblings and cousins had all been directed and obediently fallen into. But obedience had never been his strong suit.

'And was it Babs who suggested teaching?'

She shook her head. 'Oh, no. She just wanted me to choose something that would make me happy. I'm quite sporty—I like football and I coach it after school. But I'd never be able to make a living from it.'

He smiled. She smiled. He liked her. Liked how genuine she seemed. Refreshing. He had met so many women out here who were living a fast-paced life. All about the glitz and the glamour. But while she had those in spades she also had depth—and humility. Yes, definitely refreshing.

'Anyway, my first job was as a nanny, but the family wanted me to live in and I got homesick even though it was only across town. And then Babs encouraged me to aim a bit higher and I looked into teaching in a nursery. And eight years later—here I am!'

'Here you are. But you've not been here long, right? You've got absolutely no trace of sun on your skin.' She had beautiful skin. As if she bathed in cream.

'I'm really careful in the sun. It's a… There's a family issue with sun damage.'

Back to fiddling with her glass.

She looked up at the door as if she'd heard a noise but it was still quiet. He checked his phone. Sarwar had promised to call back when the raid was over and the coast was clear. Nothing.

'So what brought you out here if it wasn't the promise of third-degree burns?'

She didn't move but he sensed her tension return.

'The short version,' she began after a few moments, 'is that I came out here to be with somebody and it didn't work out.'

He thought about that for a moment. It would have

needed to be someone special to uproot her if she got homesick even in her own home town. Should he probe?

'I'm happy to listen to the long version—if you want. No worries if you don't.'

She crossed her legs. He could have sworn it was absently, unknowingly, but it gave him the best image of womanhood he'd had in a long time. The way the split in her dress sliced him a view of her toned thigh... She was hotter than the desert in July. He pulled at his collar. Was the air-con even working?

'It's not such a great story,' she said finally, and with such a sigh that he jerked his attention back to her face. 'The long version is...predictable. I fell for a guy and it turned out to be a bad decision. He... We were engaged. Then we weren't. Because he wanted to be engaged to someone else. And probably by now he's been engaged another three times over.'

Danny could *not* wrap his head around that! Getting engaged once would be one too many times for him. Where was the appeal? Why tie yourself down in marriage when the world had an endless stream of beautiful women? And why commit when you knew said women were only going to let you down?

Sure, there were people who *did* want commitment— his parents, and in all likelihood his brother Mark. That would be one wedding he wouldn't attend. But not him. He hated the idea of being stuck in the same place, doing the same thing, with the same people. Even with a beauty. It was bound to end badly.

He'd made up his mind years ago that he was not his parents. He'd wanted out—*needed* out—and he couldn't ever see himself going back. He'd moved on. Didn't want to look back. Or do a U-turn. Going back on a decision—

any decision—was a sign of weakness. As spectacularly demonstrated by Georgia's serial fiancé.

'Maybe he has shares in a diamond mine?'

'Or maybe I believe in fairytales.'

'Ah, now, don't give yourself a hard time. We all fall for the wrong people sometimes.'

He reached across to squeeze the long, elegant fingers that were rubbing the sides of her wine glass. He liked touching her. The thrum of her energy tuned him right in to her.

'I did—once. It caused a lot of damage at the time, but it was the rocket I needed to get myself out into the world. It's sore when it happens, but I bet you're already heaving a sigh of relief.'

She looked at him. Searching. He wrapped his fingers round her wrist, then smoothed little trails across her skin. She held his eyes. He looked at her lips where she'd just licked them—again. Let his gaze settle there, slow and steady. Absorbed the sensual image. *Beautiful.* He looked at her breasts. He was sure her nipples were beginning to tighten. And he began to harden. The sexual energy between them was dynamite and he hadn't even kissed her. But he would.

She looked away, took a sip of wine.

'You're right. It's much more important that I get home and get on with life.'

'So what's keeping you here?'

'Money.' She lanced him with a hard stare. 'Purely money. That probably makes me sound terrible. But it's not money for the sake of money. It's—it's Babs. I don't know why I'm telling you this, but she owes a ton of money.' She sighed. 'After years of self-sacrifice for me she met a guy. A sleazy, slimy guy. She married him and gave him a share in The Tavern. She also invested in his building firm. And when she should have been looking forward to financial security, winding down, that worthless piece of garbage conned her and robbed her and covered his tracks so well that when she tried to get back her share of the business they'd built up he had already liquidated it and started re-trading. With Babs the Younger.'

She paused and looked down at her lap. Ah, hell, if that wasn't her chin wobbling... She was trying to hide it but there was no denying the hitch in her voice and the flush over her cheeks. He moved forward, lifted her glass and put it down on the table.

She swiped a hand under each eye. 'I'm fine. Sorry—I'm fine.' She looked away and then back at him, her eyes glassy and with a fixed bright smile. 'I just miss her. I want to go home and I can't. I'm stuck here until I've earned enough to clear her debts. All sixty thousand pounds of it.'

He could no more stop himself from gathering her into his arms than stop breathing. *Selfless*. On top of every physical attribute she had she was out here to earn money for someone else. Far too nice for the likes of him.

But he understood that aching loneliness. He'd felt it when he'd got here. More than that—he'd relished it. It had proved that he'd got away, taken the first step. He knew how real it was for others, though. He loved Dubai now. Loved its pace and its vibe and its outrageous ambition. Sure sometimes, occasionally, the yearn for grey rain and green moss had him hopping on a flight home, just to inhale the sweet smell of damp Irish earth and sit for long, uncomplicated hours in the company of quiet, uncomplicated people. But as soon as his family knew he was back and started bearing down on him he hopped right back on the plane.

But Georgia Anne Blue... She was a family girl. And

she was now in the middle of a nasty piece of action that, all joking aside, could result in jail time. Of course she was emotional!

'Georgia.' He folded his arms round her but she held herself tense.

'I'm honestly fine—it's fine.'

'Sure it is. But everyone needs a little comfort sometimes. I miss my sister too. We're a long way from home. We all get lonely, Georgia.'

That seemed to undo her. She literally wilted in his arms—a flower without water. He stood her up. Her cheek landed on his chest. He scooped her closer, let his hand cradle her head and pressed his arm across her back. Steadied her and held her while she let soft sobs rack her body. She held her arms bent, tight against him, hands still in fists. Long moments of silent sadness.

'I'm sorry—I don't know where that came from.'

She pulled back a little and he felt his shirt wet with tears. That undid him. He hated to see a girl upset. In his iron-clad armour it was the one thing that could really pierce a hole. He blamed his sister Frankie for that—she always knew how to get to him.

'I know where it came from. And it's fine to let it go.'

She looked up at him, her dark green eyes glassy as a forest pool. Her lip wobbled again and she buried her head. This time she wrapped her arms around him.

'Thank you. I'm sorry.'

'Shh.' The last thing she needed to do was thank him. There was nothing he would rather do than hold her and soothe her. And his body was all the evidence she needed that he was getting payback. Holding her close was playing with fire. And he was calculating the risks attached to that right now.

He hardened—fast and fierce. He leant down and

breathed in her scent: flowers from her hair, sweet spice from her neck. He felt her body through the thin fabric of her dress as he held her. Slim, strong, soft. He dropped his arm to her waist and the sensation of the curve of her body hugged close sent him another sharp kick of lust.

She must have realised how aroused he'd got—she pulled back and looked up at him as if she was weighing up her odds, testing him for trust. He'd show her she could trust him…

It would have been nice to start slow, to brush his lips against hers and gently learn their shape. But steady and sweet had bailed out and he was riding the crest of a giant wave of lust. He snaked his hands through the thick red waves of her hair and scooped her mouth right under his. *Fierce.* He felt his body absorb the sensation of her curves. *Not enough.* His tongue took over—fired right between her open startled lips and plunged and tangled with hers.

She was shocked. Then she moaned. Then she settled even closer and her tongue met his with a hunger that fired his blood.

What a kiss.

Wild stabbing darts with their tongues—shallow at first and then duelling. Every thrust had him harder. Their mouths open wider, to taste more and more. He took and tasted her like a starving man. On and on they kissed. He heard her moan as if it was a surrender from her soul. Felt his face and her face wet from their mouths. Felt such a desperate need to feel her flesh that he dropped his hands to her full, plump cheeks and squeezed hard.

He pressed her closer and she opened her thighs to him. He ground himself against her, taking whatever pressure he could get against his length. He could feel a delicious tension start to build and knew he wa͏ control. She nestled herself hard against him, snaked he͏ arms up and gripped the back of his neck. And, oh, that let him feel those breasts against him. He put his hands on them. Right on them. Filled his hands. Felt firm, hot flesh and hard buds through the fabric. Felt as if he'd never get enough.

He stared at her dress, tugged the V apart and slid his hands inside, pulling the cup of her bra out of the way, exposing a bare white breast.

'Danny—stop!'

She pulled away and he was stunned. His head thick. An uppercut of lust to the brain. Literally reeling with what had just happened.

'I heard a noise,' she whispered, fixing her bra, closing up her dress.

He stared at her stupidly. She couldn't really want to stop this now—*could* she?

'It's all right. It's the penthouse. No one can come in.'

She stared—huge dark eyes.

'Trust me. You're safe in here.'

There was a knock at the door.

She stepped further away, looked from him to the door and back again. 'It's the police. It must be.'

'Georgia, calm down—it's fine. I told you.'

But she was panicked. The knock came again. He shook his head, walked to the door. Unlocked it and opened it. In the wide landing in front of the elevator stood two cops. No one and nothing else. They passed on the information that the place had been cleared. Sarwar had been as good as his word.

Just so long as the paps weren't hovering.

He nodded at the guys and went back inside.

'What's happening? Is it all right? Am I able to go

home now?' She was smoothing down her dress, patting her hair.

'All sorted. If that's what you want to do you can go—any time you like.'

She looked at him. 'Oh…'

He faced her, still semi-aroused. But she was elsewhere now—her mind was in a different place. Spooked.

He pulled out his phone, fumbled with the screen, irritated.

'All right.'

'*All right?* I'd like to finish our "discussion".'

She swallowed, looked at her shoes. He looked at her shoes. Red, pointed…perfect Friday night shoes.

'I…I think I should just go. I'd rather put all this behind me.'

She thought she should *go*? She could think what she wanted for now. He'd make his mind up in a little while.

'You need a lift somewhere?'

She glanced at the two discarded glasses that sat on the table. Neither of them had had any more than a sip of alcohol. 'No, thanks. My car's parked.'

'Okay.' He stood up. 'Let's head down, then.'

They left the penthouse and headed back into the elevator. The doors closed between them and the magnificent Persian Gulf. His mind was playing catch-up as he stared out at the rose-gold sun sinking fast into sapphire-blue. Diamond-white iconic buildings held shards of every other precious jewel and metal, all polished to precision and laid out for people to worship and desire. It was some town. And he was proud that his fingerprints were all over it.

They stepped out onto the fifty-ninth floor. Better not to go straight to the lobby. He wanted to see the place cleared for himself. Passed the open door of the Jumeirah Suite. There was nobody lazing or relaxing now—only empty glasses to show that anyone had been there. A vacuum.

Her shoes clicked as she walked. He put his hand out and grasped hers, squeezed it. They moved along the marble corridor to the internal elevators. Noise bubbled up from downstairs—the chatter of everyday hotel life. He still grasped her hand. Toyed with what he was going to do next.

They paused when they got to the elevators. Both stared at their fuzzy outlines in the burnished gold doors. He let go of her hand and pulled her close. But she held herself back. He hadn't expected that.

The elevator doors opened. She tucked her head down and went in.

He pressed the button and the doors closed.

'Are you okay?'

She nodded. 'Thanks.'

The elevator sped down, landed softly. She stood apart. He reached for her hand again but she shook her head.

'Danny I've… It's been… I'm grateful to you for helping me out but I just want to go home now and forget that this ever happened.'

She extended her hand for a handshake and he nearly laughed. Okay—*that* he really hadn't expected.

'No problem, Georgia. You're a lovely woman. I was happy to help.'

She shook his hand. Firmly. 'It was lovely to meet you.'

He nearly let her go at that. *Nearly.* But they'd had the hottest kiss he'd ever known. Had been heading fast to what he was sure was going to be the hottest sex. He wasn't letting her go just like that.

He pulled her up sharply, out of sight, inside the elevator. Put his mouth right over hers and kissed her the way he knew she needed to be kissed.

She wanted to say goodbye with a *handshake*?

He kissed her just long enough to have her moan and soften against him and then he pulled back. Twisted her a smile that told her she'd had a lucky escape.

But she eyeballed him, wiped her mouth. 'Bye, Danny.'

She turned on her heel. His eyes fell to her backside, swinging as she stepped away. He doubted he'd ever forget it.

And then his eyes fell on the photographers who were sitting in the lobby, cameras trained covertly. He knew it. *Oh, hell*...

He stepped forward. Grabbed her.

'Georgia, come with me.'

'I don't think so, Danny. I think we've—'

'Georgia, don't argue. There's paparazzi over there and if you don't want your picture to be going global any time, come with me. *Now*. I need to know what they know, what other pictures they've got—and so do you.'

She stared with panicked doe eyes up at him and he got that kick to his guts again. *Protect her*. He needed to protect her. He took her hand in his—no argument. Walked. Brisk. Together. Striding. Out past the fountain, the guests and the bellhops and into the darkening night.

CHAPTER THREE

JUST WHEN SHE'D thought she was in the clear. Just when she'd thought she could go home and soak away the mind-blowing night she'd just had. The shock of that party. The raid. The run. The man. *The man…*

She felt his hand wrapped round hers. Felt the firm, unyielding strength seep right into her. She walked at his side, matching his stride. Heads turned to watch them. She kept her gaze high. He drew glances and glares from the people exiting their cars and heading into the hotel. And there at the corner, where limos were disappearing to be valet-parked, was a posse of photographers.

'There are more of them,' she said, panic ringing clear in her own ears.

'Yep.'

He was focussed. Intense as the sultry night.

'Car's here.'

'I have a car.'

'I know. But we're not going to start discussing whose car we travel in now, are we? We're going to get in mine and get the hell out of here.'

For a heartbeat she wavered. She could still call the valet for her own. Get in it and head back to the complex. Close the door and hope for the best. But the change in Danny as he strode forward to the sleek black sports car was making her think that they were by no means in the clear. And though he seemed to have the police in his pocket the paparazzi were a whole different animal.

'Okay. I'll come with you.'

He raised one of those perfect brows as if to ask if there was any other choice.

Slipping into the bucket seat took her aback. So low her knees knocked against the dashboard.

He slipped his hand to the side, pressed a button that sent her seat back. 'Comfortable?'

She grasped the seatbelt that had slid itself forward and clasped it in place, looking at his face, reading it for clues. He was utterly composed. There was even a hint of a smile. But she sensed the change in him—even if he masked it better than a black veil.

'Thanks. Where are we going?'

'To limit some damage.'

'What damage?'

'That's the part I don't know yet.'

'You're saying words that scare me but you're acting as if we're off for a picnic.'

'I don't think it'll be a picnic, but there won't be anything scary.' He turned and fired his stare at her. 'Have no fear about that.'

She continued to watch the side of his face in the flare of streetlights that shone as they passed. They scooted effortlessly along Sheikh Zayed Road. Alongside the road signs and streetlights huge illuminated monoliths loomed, then passed. Taxis, SUVs and the occasional truck switched in and out of lanes. His driving, like everything else, inspired confidence, and she let herself sink back into the leather, sure that he'd be able to negotiate any of the manic moves that sometimes had to be dealt with on the roads out here.

'We're not being followed.'

She stared at him. Then turned her head to try and peer out of the tiny rear window. All she could see were lights. 'You thought we *were*? Being followed?'

He shrugged one shoulder. 'It was possible.'

Another somersault in her mind. 'Why? Who cares about *us*? Why would anyone want to follow *us*?'

His jaw was definitely tight and getting tighter. He drew in a breath, then twisted her a bemused look. 'When they've taken enough pictures of the WAGs they come looking for the rich.' His hand tightened on the wheel. 'And rich ex-pats in trouble—beautiful ex-pats in trouble—sell papers. Here *and* at home.'

'But you said we weren't in trouble!'

'With the police—no. But if those snappers have pictures of me or you anywhere near that suite then both our reputations will be in question.'

She stared. Her mouth had dropped. 'So I could still lose my job?'

He took his hand off the wheel. Laid it on her hand, resting on her thigh. Rubbed and soothed. 'Yes. You could lose your job. And I could lose myself the biggest contract I've been working towards for the last ten years. That's why we need to get our mitigation.'

He cut a swift track into another lane and took them off on a slip road to another row of illuminated sky-high obelisks. He slowed, pulled in and stopped. An avenue of palms. Staff in attendance. Another exclusive hotel.

'Public, but very restricted. Definitely no photographers. Come on.'

She was struggling to keep up but he was already out of the car and heading round it. The valet opened her door and she did her best to get out. No need as Danny hooked a hand under her elbow and steered her up and into the hotel so quickly she was sitting in a booth and sipping mineral water before she could even catch her breath.

His phone rang. He excused himself with a look and walked away, talking quickly. She watched him pace, overawed all over again. She felt as if she was playing catch-up, just being in his company. He seemed to move so fast—assured and swift. His mind raced as fast as his car. Tenacious and fiercely intelligent—you could tell just by looking at the concentration in his face even as he took his call.

So she'd thought she could climb into her own life raft and row herself to safety? Make out with the most amazing man she had ever met—*would* ever meet—and then go and soak in a tub of bubbles and chalk it down to experience?

He was too much. Too intense. That kiss had nearly blown her mind—never mind what it would do to her heart if she spent any more time with him. She had to cut loose from him. Had to let him fix whatever he was going to fix and then get him to drop her back at the hotel. Or maybe she could just pick her car up in the morning.

She shook her head, pulled out her smartphone, tapped her social media apps and started to browse.

She must have been in a state of shock. That was the only thing she could think of to explain her behaviour tonight.

Even as a child, Babs had drilled into her, *Scent trouble, head home*. And, though she'd rarely been in more trouble than choosing the wrong shade of lipstick, if she'd followed that advice tonight none of this would have happened. She should have listened to her gut the minute she'd seen that woman being pawed. Headed straight for the door and not been waylaid by Danny Ryan.

She looked at him. He was gorgeous. Utterly, unmistakably, overwhelmingly gorgeous. But that five-minute chat could cost her far more than Babs's debts.

He was still on his phone. Pacing. He spun round. Dragged a hand through his hair, then gave a fist-punch to the air. It didn't look like a celebratory one.

She scrolled through her news feed.

Oh. My. God.

This was what he was talking about. She stood up and he looked right at her. She saw him mouth some words and he was moving to her, a stern look of concern on his face, pinning her with his eyes. He clicked off his phone and pocketed it.

He reached the booth. 'What is it?'

She handed him her phone, words not coming.

He quickly flicked through it. 'Yep. It's pretty bad.'

There was a picture of them descending in the sky-lift. Hand in hand. Another showed them framed in the giant picture window of the penthouse. That kiss. Even from the distance the heat was unmistakable. It must have been taken from the neighbouring hotel roof! And it was in a stream of other pictures showing the raid, the police, the girls being arrested, others leaving the hotel.

'Thank God there are no pictures of us at the actual party. That would have been far worse.' He handed her back her phone. 'That's what my PA's checking out right now. And as far as I can tell my boys—and the company name—are out of it. So that's something at least.'

'And there's only those photos—not any of us with anyone or doing anything? So no need to worry?' She kept flicking through the media pages.

'Georgia—we're alone in a lift and in the penthouse, looking about ten seconds away from ripping each other's clothes off. One floor above that party. We're in

Dubai. I'm a name out here and you're a beauty. Face it: we're news.'

She looked up with dawning realisation of the conclusions that would be drawn by the simple fact of them being in a hotel room together.

'You know the rules about sex outside of marriage. So we have to have the same story. We were there together—no denying that. And that means we have to talk about what's next.'

He swung down into the seat opposite, the thick padding of the booth surrounding them, a flickering candle illuminating the quirk of his nose, the proud jut of his cheekbones, the determination of his mouth.

'I think we're going to have to say we were—or rather we *are*—together…a couple.'

'Why can't we just tell the truth? That we were given bad information and turned up at what we thought was a genuine party?'

'We were in an empty penthouse for an hour. We left together. They'll probably have pictures of us walking through the lobby holding hands. Do you want them to think we met there? Because I don't. Remember what's acceptable here and what's not. Mostly Emiratis turn a blind eye, but for some reason this party has attracted a lot of attention. Media attention. And I'm about to get into business bed with one of the most morally upstanding men in the whole of the Arab world. He won't want to be dealing with a guy who's all over the media for having sex outside of marriage or being at a sleazy party.'

'And you think that there's absolutely no way we can bluff it out? I just hate the idea of lying about anything.'

He steadied his stare on her. She lifted her glass to her mouth but he reached out, took it from her hands and placed it down. Took her two hands into his and held them.

'We can't say we met at a brothel, Georgia. So we have to be a couple that strayed into the wrong area. And if we are a couple exiting a hotel room we have to be married. My next venture is with Sheikh Salim. I'm due to meet with him on Sunday. Talks are at a critical point. And my face popping up in the media is not going to smooth things unless I've got an answer for every question. He'll have expectations.'

'You mean you want me to pretend to be your *wife*? Just so he'll think you're okay?'

'I mean I want you to *be* my wife. No pretence.'

His words sat between them. Impenetrable as marble. She couldn't process them. She'd been sure she couldn't be any more shocked after what she'd seen tonight. But he had just said something that blasted away another layer of her normal world.

'You heard me. I need to have an explanation for being in a hotel room with a beautiful woman in the middle of a Friday evening for when I meet with the Sheikh the day after tomorrow. I won't risk his judgement, Georgia. He would view it as complete disrespect—and I don't make a habit of disrespecting my business partners. Not when the stakes are as high as this.'

'But he'll see right through it. He… You've obviously met him before, but you've never mentioned me or said anything about having a wife. Why on earth would he believe that you're married? And, *really*? It would make *that* much difference to him?'

Danny looked to the side, to the waiter who had just appeared to top up their water. His patience rolled in waves. He sat back as bowls of uneaten snacks were removed and replaced. She watched him. He was completely composed. There was no trace of mirth playing at the corners of that mouth. His eyes were utterly, solidly focussed. He meant every word.

'You mean it, don't you? You actually think you need to do this to pull it off?'

'There's no question. You don't try to outsmart Sheikh Salim. He'll be happy knowing we're married and the rest he'll let slide. The only thing to be discussed is how quickly we can get it done.'

His phone beeped. He pulled it out. He listened. Checked his watch.

'That could work.'

He listened again. She could hear a voice talking rapidly. He nodded.

'Tell her I owe her. I'll wait to hear from you.'

The phone was clicked off again, but this time put on the table in front of them.

'It's sorted. We can go to the Irish Embassy in Abu Dhabi.' He looked at her intently. 'I'll need you to sign some papers and I'll sort out a fee for you. And I suppose we've got time to go shopping for a ring and a dress.'

'A *fee*?' He was going to *pay* her for this crazy idea?

He checked his watch again and she was suddenly struck by how expensive it was. He wore a solid gold watch. He drove a super fast car. He generated power and he exuded control. He was the Dubai dream and he wasn't going to let a silly thing like the accusation of sex out of wedlock get in his way. She was an adjunct to his plan. That was it.

She suddenly thought of Babs. What on earth would she tell her sister? That she'd gone to a singles party and wound up married? Babs—who'd thought that even her engagement to Nick after twelve months was ridiculously quick. What would she say to this?

She shook her head. It was nasty. It was duplicitous. It was about saving face and making money—not about love. Marriage was about love. It was the last fairytale she still clung on to.

'I don't want to get involved in this. I don't think things are going to be as bad as you say, and even if they are doing something as crazy as this is totally out of the question. I can't—I couldn't do it.'

He put down the glass of water he'd been drinking from. Very, very carefully. He lasered her a stare, then spoke so softly she could hardly hear him.

'I know how you feel, Georgia. Marriage is hugely important. And when the right person comes along for you this—what we're about to do—will be nothing like it—no comparison.'

He lifted one of her hands.

'Sometimes we need to do things that push our normal boundaries. But you know this is going to solve every one of your problems in one fell swoop.' He nodded at her. 'No one will get hurt. Everyone will get what they want—what they need.'

She stared at her pale fingers engulfed in his hand. Stared at where Nick's ring had sat for the three months she had stupidly, proudly worn it. A sham. A dream that had shattered like cheap plate glass. She'd sworn when she'd taken that ring off that next time—if she was lucky enough to have a next time—it would be a ring from a man with a true heart, who placed more faith in love than looks, or money.

'But there's no integrity in this. It would be a lie.'

She couldn't do it. No matter what he offered her. The one thing she had wanted her whole life was something she'd never known—a husband, a father to her children, a loving, truthful lifelong bond.

'It would be a shield, Georgia.' He laced his fingers through hers. 'A temporary, necessary shield.'

She shook her head. 'Marriage is far too important to be described as temporary—or as a shield.'

'Okay…'

Still he spoke softly, calmly. His phone buzzed. Her eyes landed on it. But he ignored it.

'Georgia.'

Her eyes switched straight back to his.

'I never intended to get married. In the real sense of the word. I still don't. And though that might make me sound like the total opposite of you I think it makes me more *like* you. It's a big deal. To me. To you. The only difference is that I don't think I'm the type for it. Or maybe I don't think there's a woman out there who'll convince me to trade what I've got now for something totally different.'

'Like monogamy?'

He shrugged. 'I don't tell anyone lies.'

'But this would be lying.'

'Georgia, there's more than my professional pride riding on this. I'm not going to go into it all now, but the stakes here are Burj-high. So you can call it lies. But I'm telling you that sometimes you have to fall on your sword for a bigger win.'

'It's *always* better to be truthful,' she stated simply.

She had to believe that or she had nothing. A quiet, scathing voice inside her reminded her that maybe her own engagement hadn't been entirely truthful, but she buried the thought as quickly as it surfaced.

'In this case it's more about respect.'

'Not for your own values, it's not.'

'Sheikh Salim's world is different to ours. I wouldn't want to offend him in any way. Georgia, it's easy—we have a ceremony in the Embassy. We visit him. He'll appreciate that—greatly. I move on with my business. You move back home. Your sister's sorted. We annul the marriage.'

'Broken down like that, it sounds like it's all in a day's work for you, doesn't it?'

'I do what needs doing.'

He cocked one perfect brow, quirked the corner of his perfect mouth. His stubble was thicker now. He looked less polished, more manly. How did anyone ever say no to him?

'No.'

He didn't frown. He sat back and smiled. His phone buzzed again. He didn't even flick it a glance.

'No is my favourite word. It's a baseline. Everything moves on from no.'

'I mean it!'

'I'm sure you do.'

'I can't—I couldn't pretend to get married. It would be wrong.'

'You wouldn't be pretending. You would be actually doing it. The only thing that would be wrong would be imagining it's a marriage in the conventional sense. It's not. It's a means to an end. It's a problem-solver. It's a moment in time.'

She felt choked, suddenly. He was impossible. She wanted to refuse and leave, but the way he was selling this was beginning to make sense. What if she could clear Babs's debts all at once? What if she could actually return home—back to The Tavern and all its comforting memories: its scents of stale beer, its sing-a-long tunes, and the regulars who'd been there almost as long as the mahogany bar top and stained glass windows.

'I'm not sure. I don't know. You're making me doubt myself.'

'That's because you know this is the only way.'

He leaned forward—trailed his fingers to her wrist. His thumb traced the faint ridge of her vein. Breath hitched in her throat.

'You've got sky-high values. I could see that the minute I saw you at the party. You're not a schemer or a plotter. You're *good*.' He laughed—a sad little chuckle. 'You've been dealt a bad hand and you're here for the duration. But, Georgia...' he lifted his hand to her face, trailed a soft caress down her cheek '...you've got a long, long shift here before you repay all that money.'

She almost preened into his touch

'And that's only if nothing comes of this media interest. That's a risk I'm not willing to take.'

His phone buzzed again. This time his eyes flashed to the screen.

'We need to make a move. Now. If we're going to pull this off.' He stood, swung in alongside her. Cupped her face with his hands. 'Trust me. I won't hurt you. I'll take care of you.'

She almost choked on the swollen sob that surged in her throat. They were words that should belong in a real marriage proposal. Words that would have her melting and sobbing a grateful yes. But this was a business marriage and a business deal. A partnership for money and her ticket back home. She'd be giving up her life here— her class of pre-schoolers, her coaching, her friends. She'd be leaving behind the memory of a broken engagement and the loneliness that came with the yawning debts and her duty to Babs.

'I'll do it,' she said.

He smiled. His eyes crinkled and flashed. He dipped his lips and planted a soft, warm kiss on her mouth.

'Good.'

He kissed her again. Just for a moment. Full on her lips. And her feral cat desire for him sprang up, startling her. What did *that* add to the mix of this fake marriage? Trouble. A crackle of warning that she'd ignored twice already.

Again she sensed it—it ignited between them like fire licking through dry straw. But although she only felt it around him she was sure that if she was in trouble he would be the one who would keep her out of the flames. And the calling, comforting, soothing energy he radiated made her feel warmth in a very dark, cold place that she'd never even realised existed before.

'We can talk on the way to the mall. Choose whatever you want for a wardrobe—for the ceremony and the days with Salim.'

He stood, threw down some bills and walked her out to collect the car. He connected the car phone as soon as they were mobile. Issued a steady stream of instructions to his PA.

He wanted all the necessary paperwork ready, gifts for the Embassy staff, a selection of rings and a contract—a pre-nup. *Of course.* He didn't even flash her a glance as he rolled out the instructions for what was to be written into it. She couldn't look at him. Even if this had been a real marriage she would have found that aspect distasteful—that someone would have so little faith or trust in her that they would think she'd ever, in a million years, want what wasn't hers.

And then he came to her own contract.

'How much do you want for this, Georgia?'

He twisted to look at her in the silence that was her

reply. She couldn't put a price on this, let alone mouth any words.

'Okay, I'll call you back with the final details.' He clicked off the call. Drove on. Slowed down. The silence continued.

'Look, I know you're not the kind of girl to strike bargains like this every day. But I'm more than willing to pay you what you need—and more.'

How could she put a price on this?

He dialled his PA back. 'A bank transfer—details to follow—made out to Georgia Anne Blue. One million sterling, payable immediately after the ceremony. A further million when the deal with Salim gets signed.'

She said nothing—just looked out of the window at the thousands of cars assembled like shiny sand beetles in the mall car park. People thronged to the doors. She'd been before—of course she had—but never with the thought of spending money in the luxury boutiques where she knew they were headed. Not even when she'd visited with Nick.

Two million pounds.

What a difference that could make to their lives. She wasn't so naive as to think it wouldn't. It was just such a shame—such an incontrovertible shame—that she had to marry a guy she'd met only hours earlier in a fake wedding to get it.

'C'mon, Georgia. It's been a night and a half. There are two shopping hours left, so let's rip through this place while we still can.'

The businessman edge to his voice had been replaced with charming, lilting tones. Soft, sensual and soothing. He placed a hand on her elbow and helped her out of his car, moved his hands to her shoulders and smiled his cutest smile.

'Where do you want to start?'

They went to her favourite Italian designer. She'd always felt too self-conscious even to go into the store back on Bond Street in London. Here it was easy—and now it seemed she might leave with a package, rather than her best vintage second-hand market finds in a recycled plastic shopping bag.

He settled himself on a sofa, drank coffee and answered calls. Scoffed fruit and sandwiches. She tried things on. Should she parade for him? Would he even care?

She decided he wouldn't and hurried her way through weekend-wear and formal. In and out of beautifully cut dresses with exquisite detailing, trousers that fitted her perfectly with light cashmere and silk tops to complement them. A butter-soft leather jacket and jewel-toned wraps. But what was she going to wear to this wedding ceremony? Little skirt suit? White froth?

She tried on a cream dress—the perfect shade for her colouring, utterly feminine with a floaty forties-style hem. Lace cap sleeves and a sweetheart neckline. A silk swathe round her bust and a lace overlay skirt. Golden and silver threads intertwined in a ribbon belt at the thinnest part of her waist.

Her hair still fell in waves, and even though her makeup was nearly gone and dark circles had formed under her eyes she felt that she looked good.

'Georgia?'

She hesitated then walked out to see what he wanted. After all, it wasn't as if she needed to protect herself from bad luck.

He was distracted—the fingers of one hand whirring across his tablet keys, a cup of coffee in the other hand. He glanced up.

'We need to step on it.'

'Okay,' she said simply, and turned to go.

'Wait.'

She stilled at his voice—the tone was less a command than an entreaty.

When she turned back to see what he wanted he was moving to his feet.

She was used to men looking at her—mostly across the bar in The Tavern or on the soccer pitch at her after-school training. She didn't really mind and she never reciprocated. But the lick of lust she suddenly saw in Danny's eyes startled her. He clattered down his coffee cup. So he wasn't in complete control... She was glad. Suddenly she realised she wanted him to want her. She *badly* wanted him to want her. She felt her power, felt less like a pawn in his game. He needed her to pull this off, and right now he looked as if he needed her at some much more primal level too.

She dropped her arms.

He swallowed.

'You look...beautiful.'

She dipped her eyes and smiled her thanks. Retreated back into the changing room, turned and faced the free-standing mirror. He came up behind her, as she had known he would. Her eyes and his met in the mirror. Then his hands were on her shoulders. Lightly skimming down her bare arms. Up, down...gentle, caressing.

He stepped a little closer. She knew he was going to dip and kiss the stretch of skin from collarbone to earlobe and she ached for it. Her belly contracted and her nipples hardened. From her mouth came a hushed, sensual sigh. Back tipped her head...heavy. His lips and then his teeth found the most sensitive, aching spot and licked...and bit. She sank back into him and his arms engulfed her.

'Georgia. You drive me wild.'

Those words…those arms…that mouth. Had she known how those few simple things could utterly transport her she would never, *ever* have agreed to marry Nick. She would have known how lacking he was. Worlds apart.

She wanted more than anything to feel Danny turn her in his arms and make love to her. She twisted round. He was strong, unyielding. He moulded her to him. Hands swooped and worked her just where she needed them.

Then he stopped and stepped back. Drew a heavy breath in, then out. 'Not yet. We can't.'

She stared with glazed eyes.

'I know. I get it. We have to be married first.'

How crazy was that? He hitched half a smile and she turned away—but he grabbed her. Cupped her face and pulled her so close to him the breath in her chest was forced out. He covered her mouth, thrust in his tongue as if in a claim and took her with absolute mastery.

As quickly he released her, and she staggered back.

'Buy that dress. It's perfect.'

He looked at her, painting desire all over her. She stared back at him, almost breathless, taking in every inch of his tall, broad-shouldered body. Three buttons undone at his neck, shirtsleeves loosened…muscle, power and total control. But her eye caught the pulse at his throat—and it hammered just like hers.

It was like a stand-off of desire.

'Have you got lingerie? You'll need that too.' His eyes never left hers as he growled out the words.

Scenes played out in her mind. Kept her rooted, staring, longing.

'Have we got time? The shops will shut at midnight. And then what do we do? Where do we go?'

It brought him back to business. He started to rub his face. 'This is going to work. It *is*. Right... Let's think it through.'

He turned to her.

'Get dressed—quickly. We need an engagement ring. The rest can wait. I'll get stuff sent to my home. No, not my home—we can't go there. We need to be out. We need to court the paparazzi and give this story some legs.'

Story. That was all it was. For a moment she'd been caught up in the glamour and excitement. For a moment she'd felt as if he really had feelings for her. He'd seemed almost out of control before he'd called it back in check. But he was tense—as tense as she'd seen him. *She* wanted to soothe *him* this time. Tell him it was all going to be all right.

But this was a simple business deal. She was being project-managed. All she was was a factor. A factor he had to dress up and parade about to lend his project some kudos. But a factor that he didn't have the ultimate say over—she was her own boss. And she mustn't forget it.

She joined him moments later in the uncrushable Alaïa dress. She could have stepped out in some of the new stuff. But she needed something to remind her of who she was in all this crazy maelstrom of shopping and weddings and trips to meet a sheikh. And a twenty-year-old stretchy dress from a market in Notting Hill was about as grounded as it got.

Credit cards swiped and bright smiles exchanged with the sales staff she left the boutique and tripped alongside him to the jewellers. Just when she'd thought Dubai couldn't get any more surreal they were off to shop for a diamond.

They strode across polished marble, past miniature fountains and embellished pillared entrances. Every click of her scarlet slingbacks reminded her just how much her life had changed since she'd slipped out of the complex a few hours earlier.

She hadn't answered the messages from her friends that had started piling in. What would she say? The only one she'd opened had been from Kirsty, apologising profusely for suggesting the Al-Jafar party. It had been a social media invite she'd seen and passed on. A social media disaster that Georgia was now living.

In the velvety hush of De Beers she stared at the trays he'd commanded be spread out for her. Her eyes widened at the blinding rainbow beauty. Dazzling. To die for. But her heart was just a tiny bit crushed. Her once treasured solitaire was like a speck of glitter compared to these. But at least she had received it in good faith. That moment when she had opened the ring box had been so full of hope and promise. As if all her dreams were contained within it.

She knew now that her instincts had warned her then that the marriage should not be more important than the man. A dark little voice had whispered that marriage might bring her the dream life of husband, children and the security she craved, but what was she trading in return?

Still, even that had seemed much more real than this.

'You must be so happy, madam,' the dreamy-eyed salesgirl gushed.

Danny had walked away on a call. Georgia's eyes had followed him, as they always did—as all women's eyes did.

Tall, proud, commanding. His low lilting burr issued instructions and seduced her senses, made her feel drowsy with lust. She was drawn to listen in awe, just wondering at how easily he could own words and fill space. And then he turned and she saw those eyes and she was even more tangled up in him than ever.

This was going from dangerous to treacherous. She was choosing a ring to wear that would tell the world he was hers and she was his. And, though they were both clear on their motivations, her soft little heart had just felt a pop of hope that this might actually be real.

She smiled back at the salesgirl. It would be real for Babs when she gave her a cheque to clear the black hole of debt.

'Yes, you're right—I'm over the moon.'

CHAPTER FOUR

AFTER A NIGHT in another luxury hotel, during which Georgia had barely slept despite the fact that her husband-to-be was in the neighbouring room, she now found herself on his company's private jet. In the air. Heading to be married. The Irish Embassy in Abu Dhabi the venue.

Nothing seemed to be a problem. Passports, forms, ambassadorial staff. All had been ticked off the rapidly growing list. Questions posed—answers given, all in that low, calm, composed burr.

The only question *she* didn't have an answer for was how she was going to manage her rapidly growing attraction to him. Every move he made, small or large, drew her eye. And he knew it. He'd caught her. And every time he had he'd flashed her a glimpse of that sinful smile.

But this was new territory for her. She'd never been very physical with anyone before. She certainly didn't do half the stuff her girlfriends got up to, and with every passing moment in his company she was getting bolder and bolder. She really needed to find her limit—and soon. Danny didn't seem to have any difficulty managing *his* attraction. Even in modest Dubai he'd held her hand, draped a casual arm over her and, when he'd been sure they were totally unobserved, had kissed her.

Kissed her. And she knew in her heart that she'd never

experience kisses like them again. He simply shook her apart every time he put his lips on hers. Supplication. Then payback. She learned his way and she gave it right back. And he took it and loved it. Stared into her eyes for long moments while the world righted itself and then smiled at her. That smile. Oh, boy, she was going to get herself into a lot more trouble than jail-time if she didn't stop thinking this was real.

'Ready?'

He'd just caught her again. It was possible she'd actually had drool spilling from her mouth. She really needed to get a hold of herself.

''Course I'm ready.'

Though that was a downright lie. They'd been up in the air for about ten seconds, it seemed, on the one-hundred-and-fifty-kilometre flight between the two cities. And she'd needed every second to settle her head and her nerves.

It was still incredible. Usually on a Saturday afternoon she'd be looking forward to a night out with the girls. She'd be finishing a coaching session, hanging back at the end to soothe the anxieties of rich parents who worried that their children might not become world-class soccer players. The parents were the hardest part of her job. They had no idea how much they let their worries influence their children. When she had children she'd do her utmost to nurture them for who they were—not who she wanted them to be.

When she had children...

The plane dipped in a little pocket of turbulence and with it her stomach as she suddenly thought of herself as a parent. Another look at Danny. And a swell of sadness that it wouldn't be with him.

No. He was most definitely not the marrying type, ironically. He was the lifetime-commitment-to-winning type. She'd already realised that his quietly composed manner hid a power furnace of energy and drive. Even in the elevator she'd felt it, seen it. Immediate deferral to his will by…*everybody.* Even by her in agreeing to this marriage.

And, though he'd had to drag that agreement out of her, with each moment she spent in his company more and more tiny little bubbles of happiness were forming all by themselves, and she was struggling to keep on top of popping them.

Oh, yes, she was in trouble.

They exited into a waiting car. As soon as they were inside he reached across the leather for her hand and squeezed. Then the smile. Another bubble. *Pop!*

She turned away and looked out of the window at the searing blue that Kitemarked every day in the United Arab Emirates. But not as searing a blue as the eyes that pinned her now as he turned her cheek with a soft, firm touch.

'Are you all right?'

He still hadn't shaved, so the stubble was even thicker—almost a beard now. Meaning that his wine-dark lips and gleaming teeth were shown in even greater contrast. There was nowhere to turn. She might as well give in.

'I'm good. Thanks. You?'

He nodded. 'I know it's not how you imagined your wedding would be, but please don't think of it like that. It's just a step forward. And you'll be doing so much more good than you even realise.'

He leaned forward. She ached to kiss him.

'And you'll be shot of me in no time.'

She smiled. 'The sooner the better,' she said. And she meant it. She really did.

Danny was finding this hard. She was the sweetest girl, and he was using her so badly. All her little-girl fairytales were caught up in weddings and husbands and all that jazz. And here they were performing a business transaction. But a very *necessary* business transaction. Salim's people had been in touch asking questions already. He'd done his homework and he knew they really were going to have to pull this off.

He'd waited a while, to see just how much media interest there was in the Al-Jafar party story. One word: plenty. At least he'd managed to cultivate some distance between himself and the other guys who'd got themselves lifted by the cops. Thankfully none of *his* boys— though that was down to Sarwar, for sure. So far the only comments he'd seen surrounding him and Georgia were speculation.

What was one of Dubai's most eligible bachelors doing with a mystery woman, near the scene of a busted party?

Looking for his sanity, he felt like posting, *after losing it to an auburn-haired temptress*. He was sure he'd have been more on the ball if his sense hadn't been kicked to the kerb the minute he saw her.

But he'd lost it for sure. And now he'd reaped the consequences. *That's what happens, Ryan, when you chase women ahead of business*. But at least he had an out— and a rapidly forming plan. Beginning with planting a few comments via his PR department. *'Secret romance for Dubai's engineering mogul'* and *'Rumours of an imminent announcement'* ought to do the trick.

The only downside was that his family were going to

be reading them along with the rest of the world. He'd emailed his sister Frankie to forewarn her and she'd responded in typical Frankie style with a launch at his judgement, values, intelligence, wit and appearance. She was nothing if not consistent. God, he missed her.

The thought of any guy using Frankie the way he was about to use Georgia twisted at his gut. He felt bad about it—he really did. But she was going to be well rewarded, and the only damage she should suffer was a wrecking ball through another fairytale castle. She'd meet a nice guy and the fact that she'd chalked up one failed engagement and one annulled marriage wouldn't matter—not if he loved her.

Now *there* were some words that tasted bad. Acidic.

He leaned over. Only one way to get sweetness back in his mouth. He pulled her close.

He was rapidly growing to need one of these kisses every five or ten minutes. He closed his lips over hers. Slowly touched, then sleekly tasted. Beautiful. Another. She just knocked him out. Every time. He was almost permanently aroused around her.

Annulling the marriage…? That would be on the assumption that it wasn't consummated. And that seemed less and less likely by the second.

Not for the first time he counted his blessings that this whole unfortunate incident had happened with Georgia and not some other woman he'd taken a momentary interest in. At least she'd played it straight so far. He instinctively felt he could trust her, as well as lust after her. And he had no doubt whatsoever that she would be as happy to say goodbye to him as he would to her.

And who was to say they couldn't use this time for fun? Like right now—the ride to the Embassy would take longer than the flight had, and they were shielded from the world here in the back of the limo. Tinted glass and muted sound.

That thought ran through his head as he leaned in for another kiss. Might be ages until they were completely in private again…

It was like a breaking wave—the way his desire for her crashed through him. Even when he could feel it coming he was powerless against it when he got so close to her. His mouth moved over hers again. And again. The soft wet heat of her…the way her tongue meshed and melded with his. The way she melted into him and then sparred with him.

His hands just had to be full of her. That silken hair… those supple arms. And although he was trying—he really was—not to slip his hands beneath her silk T-shirt, he just had to unhook her bra. *Had to*. He knew what was going to happen next, but they were on fire for each other and there was no one here to see them.

'Georgia…'

He pulled up her T-shirt and shifted her bra. Such perfect full breasts. He stroked and touched and palmed. Felt her nipples harden sharply. He wanted everything—he dragged his head to her soft sweet flesh and suckled hard.

'Danny! Oh—that's perfect!' She held his head against her nakedness, ran her fingers through his hair and began to moan her pleasure.

He wanted to give her more. Could they make love in the car and get away with it? He tried hard to get the heavy sensual fog to clear but he was still drowning in her.

'I want to touch you. Danny…I need to.…'

She ran her hands down and over his chest and abs. Her fingers flew to his belt. She was going for it. Another surge of lust and he swelled even more. He felt her fingers unbuckle, unzip, and finally close around him. She looked up, those eyes full of shade and light, trust and promise. He couldn't hold her gaze. Had to let his head fall back, adore her touch. She was incredible. She gripped him and stroked him and inflamed the sweet heat in him. Closer and closer.

The car rolled to a halt. They had to stop. *Had to.*

With all his strength he lifted his head, met her eyes, wide and wild with her own actions—as if she was out of control herself.

He heard footsteps and voices. He pulled her away, shielded her. Hooked her bra, pulled her T-shirt down. She smoothed her hair. The door opened. She climbed across him, stepped out.

'Mr Ryan is just finishing a call. He'll be with us in a moment or two.'

She closed the door and he sat back—right back. Head back. *Hell!* He was still unzipped. His legs were shaking and he'd lost the use of his arms. And the use of his brain. Things were getting out of hand. He'd been given a get-out-of-jail-free card and he was still acting like an adrenalin junkie, a teenager. A class-A idiot.

Quickly he fastened himself. Rubbed a hand through his hair and shook his head. *Finishing a call.* He had to laugh. So she was quick off the draw too. Useful in a wife….

He'd been to weddings. Cousins'. Friends'. That sort of thing. He was of that age group now where fewer and fewer were left standing. At least none of his siblings had fallen yet. And he was known—not only to himself—as the one least likely to.

He'd given the subject no more thought than that. It was filed in a pending part of his brain along with other files, such as retirement and golf. He knew the rudiments—who didn't? But once again everything where Georgia Blue was concerned tipped him into some other universe, where normal rules and behaviour didn't apply.

He should not be standing gawping at her. He should not be feeling any emotion. This was cold-blooded business. He definitely should not be reading anything more into this than what it was.

But he couldn't help himself.

The moment he saw her walk towards him from the room they had set aside for her to change into that cream dress he kissed goodbye to all composure.

Breathtaking. Beautiful.

She walked to stand beside him beaming—not with a smile, but with radiance. Like autumn sunbeams through a forest canopy.

She was fragile, but strong. Smaller, yet equal. Every part of him warmed to her.

The Ambassador spoke some words. That was as much as he heard. He was tuned in to her and nothing else. She smiled at him and nudged him to read from the card he'd been handed. That was fine in principle, but something had happened to his voice.

He said what he had to say. She responded. Said her own vows. He wasn't listening to them. Didn't want to hear them. This was all feeling too real.

Another nudge—this time for the ring. No, *not* shaky hands. No way. He held her fingers in his. Pale, tapered, with small neat nails. The engagement ring she'd been almost forced to accept was on her other hand now. The simple band of gold slid on.

He looked at her. She looked at him. And his heart burst. Slumberous, trusting eyes stared back at him. *Oh, hell.* No frivolous or flippant smile as she found his ring and slid it on. He tried to smile, to lighten things. He really did. But when he looked at her again all he felt was that this was wrong, and yet right. He shouldn't be messing with values like this. Shouldn't be making a lie of one of the most important things in life. But, strangely, it wasn't the wrongness that had sent him flying with a heavyweight hook—it was the almost terrifying sense of rightness.

He knew it was time to kiss her when she slid her hands up onto his shoulders. She was smiling now. A big toothy grin that balanced her from elegant beauty to girl next door. But she was also wobbling.

He leant down. He kissed her. Softly. Sent her trust with his lips. Succour. But still the lurking sensual flames licked round them.

He pulled back. Now was not the time to get lost in her. He had to be feeling like this because of what she'd done to him in the car. Another boundry crossed. A deeper level of trust. So maybe the best thing would be to put a bit more distance between them anyway. If he was to get his sanity back. He'd need that very soon. Salim was sharp as a drawer full of tacks. And even though he could easily explain away his foggy brain with his newlywed cover, he'd need to have every aspect of his story—*their* story—straight so as not to be caught out. Not to mention his life's work—the billion dollar deal that was still shimmering like a mirage.

'You okay?'

She nodded, but he noticed she kept her eyes trained away. She smiled, but not at him. Ursula, the Ambassador, wife of a personal friend with whom he'd so far managed to avoid getting into conversation, was congratulating her. Whispering to her in the conspiratorial way women had. About him. For sure.

He moved away, shook a few hands and got a fair few whacks on the back. *Dark horse. Lucky guy. Who'd have thought it*? Yep. Who'd have thought it, right enough.

He was handed a glass of something. Nearly necked it but put it down. It really was time to get back in the game. This was done. The next thing on the list was travelling back to Dubai to spend the night there. Then they'd be up early and on to Salim's palace—because that was what it was.

Even though he was a modest man, with modest tastes, who spent most of his time in a small private villa in Dubai, he liked to entertain his guests in style. And that meant that the next few days of high-powered business talks would be conducted in his vast palace in the desert.

Danny looked at Georgia. He would be throwing her to the wolves there too. He hadn't properly worked through that part yet. Yes, they were married now—cover intact, respect complete—but she might be quizzed or, worse, disdained. He hadn't really talked over with her the fact that she would be on her own with the other women a fair bit. He'd been so focussed on the prize. On finally getting his hands on this contract.

He paced over to her, slid his arm around her waist. Felt the electricity leap off her. 'Georgia, we'll need to leave shortly.'

She nodded, 'Of course. I'll start to say my good-byes, then.'

She slipped out of his grasp and he watched her move across the room, her movements fluid and confident, her head high. She spoke to the assembled staff, thanked them warmly. Earned herself a hug from the Ambassador and benign looks from the old guard. From the younger guys it was a different story. They were openly admiring. Eyes trailing all over her. She was innocently, charmingly chatting and their eyes were lapping her up. He could feel a burning in his gut. He wanted her away from them.

He growled her name.

She turned, almost startled. As did the rest of the room. Then she held up her finger, as if he were one of her little pre-schoolers, before going back to her schmoozing.

He had to draw in a breath to steady himself. It had been a long time since he'd felt a sudden swell of jealousy as fierce as that. He'd thought he'd buried those urges for ever. This was not good. Not good at all.

Fourteen years out of Ireland—fourteen years to master every last impulse that had dragged him down, those angry rages he had taken against his brother until the last one. Belittling behaviour that he'd loathed but hadn't been able to control—at the time. But out here he'd done it. He was his own boss, with no comparisons to anyone, no family name to live down, no reputation to uphold.

And he'd be damned if he'd let himself slide back into any of that. No way. This was a warning to him. A well-timed, well-placed warning. He was letting emotion get back in the ring. Having his head turned by a beautiful woman. Lust over logic. And now jealousy—the worst sparring partner of all.

He turned on his heel. He'd get the car, get them back to the airport, get back in the game. Georgia was playing a part and that was it. She was an attractive woman—a very attractive woman—but that was all she was. After the trip she'd be going her way and he'd be going his. But first would come the not inconsequential round of talks with the Sheikh—that was where it was at.

'Danny, wait!'

He heard her as he felt her. Her hand sneaked through his arm.

'Sorry if I took too long—they were all so *nice*. Throwing us that little reception... Did you get something to eat? I can't believe they got that fabulous buffet ready in time—and I loved it that they did English ham and Irish soda bread sandwiches! And Ursula is so nice—it was lovely of her to come in and marry us. I wanted to thank her...'

'She was told to. By her husband. It wasn't a big romantic gesture, Georgia. No big deal—just a favour called in so we can get on with the charade—nothing else. So let's get on to the next bit and show the world our fake wedding night.'

He saw the impact of his words straight away. Her face was wiped clean of its sunshine.

'Sorry. I'm sorry.' He shook his head, felt his teeth clamp together. He was still in thrall to this rage.

She stepped back...away. 'Of course. I know. I was just...'

He breathed through his clenched teeth, unfurled his fists and dredged every last bit of composure up from the murky depths he'd been plumbing.

'You were just being nice. You were being pleasant and I was being an idiot.'

She was digging deep for pride—he could see it. Colour had flushed over her cheeks and her eyes had flitted to the floor. But her spine was straight and her shoulders were back. A smile worked free, and an almost-laugh.

'You said it! Shall we go, then? On with the party? Though can I suggest you lose the angry look?'

'Yeah, I've got it. I'm worse than your four-year-olds.'

She fixed her happy face and nodded, and he could see that she was an actress on top of all her other talents. Behind the cute grin there was a splintered smile. He'd cut her off and cut her up, but she was playing the part a good deal better than he was.

He tried to put his arm round her, tuck her close to him by way of apology, and she played along—right until they'd said their final goodbye and stepped back inside the car. And then it really hit him what he'd done.

Her poker spine and her poker face were turned straight ahead. Her hands were on her lap and her knees were locked together. And the air between them was colder than the frozen air-con that plagued every indoor space in the Emirates.

'We'll be back at the airport soon.'

Perhaps she nodded. She certainly didn't speak.

'I'd better brief you on what to expect tonight and to-morrow. It might not be quite like the party we've just had.'

She answered him by sliding the rings off. First one. Then the other. She opened the catch of her little silk purse, then pulled out a drawstring bag—tiny, only big enough for the rings. He watched, unable to speak because he couldn't quite form thoughts into sentences.

'I'm sure there will be time enough to brief me later. I'd really like to close my eyes. Just for five minutes.'

He lifted her hand. He couldn't help it. Rubbed at where the rings had been. The simple band of gold had slid on so easily. Slid off so easily too.

'You know you'll need to keep them on?'

Her eyes were closed and she'd tipped back her head. 'I know.'

'So what...? Why take them off just now? Are they too tight? Too loose?'

A long, deep sigh.

'Too much. They're too much. *You're* too much. It's

all too much.' Her voice was light, eyes still closed. 'Just give me a little space, Danny. I'm beat.'

She was right. Completely right.

'Sure.'

That would be the ideal thing to do. Give each other a bit of space. Let him get a hold of himself again. Focus. Direction.

Georgia and the whole wedding thing was a bit of frippery to smooth things over. This deal—this two-billion-dollar deal—was where it was at. Getting tucked up with Salim had been years in the making. Getting work for his boys and, even sweeter, making inroads for the immigrant manual workers. *That* was where his focus should be—completely.

But the fact was that now he had this new variable to deal with—Georgia. He'd never factored that into his risk assessment. It had been *his* vision, *his* plan, *his* way the whole way. Those things he could control. And, though he'd had the brainwave to turn the problem of the party into the solution of the marriage, he'd need to use what was left of this time to work out every last angle that might come at them.

Because although he might be the consummate risk-manager—although he might be the master manipulator of all the variables—the one thing he'd just realised he *didn't* have complete control of was himself. Or her—the stunning redhead. Though she seemed to be completely herself. And add to the mix his temper—that was a wild card he really didn't want to play.

The car rolled on through the skyscraper-lined streets. Blistering heat outside. Glacial silence inside. She sat in her beauty, mutely composed. He kicked out his legs, feeling once again like the angry little boy who didn't measure up. *Damn it to hell.* He'd get a hold of himself.

He'd make sure his attraction to her was stifled until he had exactly what he wanted.

Fourteen years was a long time to learn patience… to wait for his reward. No redhead was going to unravel him now. Not even this one.

CHAPTER FIVE

'I'VE ARRANGED FOR a few friends to join us later at Indigo. Does that suit?'

She sipped at her tea, took her time replacing the cup
in the saucer. Finally she said, 'Of course.'

He barely looked up from his tablet.

Imagine being his actual wife, Georgia thought. The
contrast in his moods was worse than the contrast in the
temperature. All over her like spilled whisky one minute
and then frozen like a daiquiri sour the next.

'Would you like me to pretend to be *happily* married
or just married?'

He looked up then. Flicked over the screen of his tablet and zapped her with that laser-blue stare. 'It would
be best if you could pretend to be both. Is that possible?'

She shrugged. She was still tired. Still fed-up. She'd
played along—stupidly played along—but she was all
out of puff and there was still their 'wedding night' to
live through. Here, in the outrageously luxurious boutique hotel that was to be their home for the next twenty-
four hours.

She had chosen to disengage her emotions while she
went through the motions of changing from the cream
gown into a silk tunic and skinny jeans combo. She had
barely registered the lushly planted private courtyard gar-

den and pool, the elegant Art Deco furnishings—*genuine* Art Deco, she'd been assured. She *had* noticed the bed, but more as if it was an exhibit in a museum than something she would actually be sleeping in—alone.

He had considerately stayed out of the way, making calls and doing whatever other high-powered activities he did while she changed. But now they were facing each other across a large linen draped table in the private dining area, she stirring lemon round in an iced tea and he tap-tap-tapping away about who knew what.

'I know today's been difficult. I…I've been difficult.'

He turned his power furnace down from *scorch* to *soothe*. She was getting used to recognising how the lilting tones softened and settled when he was relaxed. Or in control. Because she'd witnessed first-hand what happened when all his little ducks didn't line up just the way he wanted them.

'Yes, you have.' She wasn't going to roll over like everyone else seemed to. He had been ill-mannered. Almost rude. She wouldn't put up with that from a class of four-year-olds, and she wasn't going to gloss over it for him—even for the short time she was going to be with him. Even for a two-million-pound pay cheque.

He smiled his cutest smile, reached out his hand and squeezed hers. That smile must have got him out of so much trouble.

'I'll make it up to you. We'll have ourselves a great party tonight.'

'You mean a dinner party? Isn't that going to look a bit odd? I mean, you've gone to great lengths to create a cover story. But who gets married and then goes out for dinner? Even if it *is* to one of the best restaurants in the world.'

'The cover story is fine. We're in love. We couldn't

wait to get our families here so the celebration dinner is with a small group of friends. Yours are out of town. It's not going to last all night and we *have* to do something public. Plus, the Sheikh is going to throw us an Emirati reception when we get there tomorrow. We'll release some pictures of that. I'll get the business dealt with and then we'll be heading off on honeymoon—except we'll be able to shelve that by then, of course.'

'Of course,' she repeated blandly.

'We can fly to London, visit your sister, and then I'll head over to Ireland. I doubt very much that the paps will still be following us at that point. And with Salim's deal in the bag it'll be fine to start our separation as soon as we're out of the limelight. How does that sound?'

'It sounds like you've got everything planned down to the last detail.'

He nodded. 'That's how I like it. No surprises. Nothing left to chance.'

'Of course there *is* the issue that Sheikh Salim hasn't actually signed your contract yet.'

He frowned—just a little. 'True. But I'm an optimist. I've got to be. No point sweating about it now. I've worked for this for three years and I've even got married because of it!'

He smiled and chuckled. Charm just oozed. She smiled back, despite herself.

'I know,' she said. 'I was there.'

He almost winked at her. 'You were a beautiful bride. You nailed it.'

'I suppose as compliments go that's a one-off.'

Suddenly he looked serious. 'Georgia, I know how much the institution of marriage means to you. And I'm not belittling it. But what we did…today…was a means to a very big end.'

She looked down. It still didn't sit right with her. It was murky and unpleasant. A lie.

'Look at it another way. If you hadn't done it—if we'd brazened it out—there's a good chance you'd have lost your job by now. You might have been deported—or, worse, jailed. That would have made it pretty hard to clear up your sister's debts. And there's no point in pretending—they would have been harder on you than on me. It's a fact of life.'

The misery inherent in that particular outcome wasn't lost to her. She stirred her lemon round and round again.

'So what do you want to do for the next few hours? Shop? Swim?' He opened the lid of his tablet again. 'I've got a few things to deal with and then I can join you. Whatever you want?'

She picked up the brochure she'd been flicking through.

'I've already booked myself the Honeymoon Spa. It's supposed to be a couples' experience, but I'm sure they'll understand if you'd rather spend time with your emails.'

She didn't mean it to sound snippy but maybe it had come out that way…a bit. He laughed. A proper rich laugh. And it even reached his eyes. He stretched his hand across and intertwined his fingers with hers.

'You're absolutely right. It's not a good look. I'm supposed to be enjoying myself with my beautiful bride.'

'Yeah, maybe stick your "out of office" on with—*I will reply to your email on my return from the Honeymoon Spa.* Otherwise your cover might be blown.'

He chuckled again. 'You don't know my colleagues. They wouldn't be surprised if I emailed in between speeches at my *real* wedding. I'm not known for my love of downtime.'

My real wedding. She hated that those words hurt

her—just a tiny bit. Of *course* this wasn't a real wedding to him. Of *course* it was just a charade to secure a contract. And why on earth anyone would want to marry a man who was already married—to his job—was beyond her. But as she looked at her fingers in his, with the rings now back in place at his insistence—all part of the public charade, she couldn't help releasing another of those little happiness bubbles.

'So…Honeymoon Spa! I'd love to come.'

He picked up the brochure. Skimmed through the pages.

'*"A rub of crushed cocoa beans"*. Sounds delicious.'

He stood up. Began to gather her towards him. His eyes told her he wanted her.

'I'm hungry.'

He did like to kiss and be kissed. That was for sure. She could live with that. He pulled her in close. She could definitely live with that. He covered her mouth with his firm soft lips. Oh, yes, even if it was only for another few days.

They walked round to the spa, hand in hand. He paused at the heavy mahogany door of the female changing area. Ran a finger down her cheek and smiled that darkly sinful smile he could pull from his repertoire so easily, so evocatively.

She shivered. A curl of lust unfurled from her core. *He knew.*

He opened the door for her and she slipped inside—away from him. Her clothes she folded and tucked away. She wrapped herself in the hugest, softest robe she'd ever seen and then stood, like a dumb doll, staring at herself in the mirror. What was she *doing*? The knowledge of her nudity and his under their robes was making her throb with sensual longing. Her excitement was growing and she wasn't even near him. She was succumbing more and more easily to just a look or a thought of him. And it was only going to lead to trouble.

He was a man. He was built to have fun and move on. His heart was hardened to love and his brain was attuned to winning. He was immune. And even if he felt anything like what she felt, where was it going to go? Nowhere. He had been crystal-clear about what was going to happen over the next few days. And the fact that he found her sexually attractive no doubt simply added an extra layer of sugar to his sweet little deal.

She looked at herself, at the gaping neckline of the robe. Shortly she'd be lying on a massage bed, next to him, naked. Where was *that* going to lead? And could her bruised heart withstand it? Well, there was no choice—it had to. She simply had to act as he did. Like a man. As if this was a fling to be enjoyed and then dispensed with. The silver lining of her fake wedding cloud. It was that simple.

She pulled open the door.

'Hey, wife.'

He leaned against the wall, the leader of the pack. He reached out for her hand, tucked it close to his side.

They entered the spa room together, to meet their masseuses and prepare themselves. For a moment they were left alone to disrobe.

He touched his belt. 'I'm not going to lie to you, Georgia. I'm going to find this quite a challenge.'

'A challenge?'

'To keep things…appropriate.' When she didn't get it he added gruffly, 'To keep my hands off you.'

'Oh,' she breathed, very aware of the heavy sensual fog in the room. The essential oils and the musk of desire. She would have to rise to the challenge of keeping it 'appropriate' too. 'Well, let's try hard, okay?'

She walked to one of the beds, sat with her back to him and shrugged the robe off. She slipped up onto the bed under a giant towel and lay down. Stuck her face through the cushioned gap and stared at the glass-covered turquoise water—her very own square metre of Gulf—flowing beneath her. She would keep this appropriate if it killed her.

The masseuses re-entered and padded forward on bare feet. Barely aware of their shadows and shapes, she felt herself succumb to the scents and soothing sounds that swirled around her. Their hands worked in choreographed union, smoothing over flesh, easing aches and rendering her senses replete.

Heavenly.

She let all the trials of the past few hours spill away with every sweep of those hands. Her breathing slowed. Her mind cleared. Her body relaxed.

Danny was there. She didn't even have to look to know exactly what he looked like spread out on the bed. His long sun-and-hair-darkened legs slightly apart and lying loose. A tiny towel covering his rock-solid rear. The hands of the masseuse would be easing oil into the flesh of his back. Muscles rippling with each sweep.

She felt as if she was out of her body, floating above him…watching. She almost saw the clever hands work down past his waist. The towel being rolled down. And there he was—almost completely naked. Paler skin. Fingers kneaded his firm gluteus muscles. One side. Then the other. He lay god-like. Then his calves. In and around the muscle. Over and up the back of his hair-roughened thighs. His legs shifted open slightly more, a dark shadow at their apex. She felt the desire to touch him, to absorb every scent, to hold him against her...

Appropriate. The word sprang into her mind as if he had just whispered it. She sank back into her own moment. Felt her own flesh relax and soften.

Minutes later she heard the whispered tones of the masseuse. They would be left alone now. Refreshments would be waiting outside if they wished.

She heard the light slip-slap of their feet on the floor and the door close. Her senses soared like a jet above the clouds. She was suddenly and completely awake.

She heard a louder noise—a click—a lock turning. Her head twisted, her neck still like soft putty. He was at the door. Naked. Her eyes feasted on his masculine beauty. Every limb and muscle glistening. He turned. He was already very erect. She felt her heart thunder and her blood course in readiness.

He walked towards her, slowly. She absorbed every single moment.

'Turn round. I want to look at you.'

The word 'appropriate' flew out of her brain. She turned. Without question.

The towel covered her, skimmed her thighs and the very tips of her breasts. She leaned up on her elbows. He leaned down.

'Did you enjoy that?'

She nodded. 'It was fabulous. I'm so relaxed now. So...relaxed.'

His arousal was huge, perfect, utterly disarming. She could focus on nothing else.

'I almost felt that those were your hands on my skin.'

She knew exactly what he meant. It felt almost spiritual—they were so in tune.

He looked down at her. At the tiny tangle of curls that peeped from the white towel.

'Open your legs. A little wider.'

An insolent command but she immediately complied. The towel slipped higher.

'That oil on your legs looks good. Smells good. All the way up to your hips—you have such white, soft skin, Georgia.'

She couldn't answer. She was so, so ready. Never, ever had she laid herself out like this for anyone. She was a girl who held back, modest to the last. And here she was, freed from all her good-girl inhibitions, spread out like a banquet, sure that she would do anything for him.

He came closer. Lifted one leg, kissed her calf—roughly. Then suddenly he turned those laser-like eyes on hers. Sent a fiery flare to her heart. He placed her ankle on his shoulder and bent his head. Slowly, slowly… Eyes still burning hers, he breathed down to her knee—inside.

Her head fell back as he started a flame trail round and down with his tongue. Then to the other leg, which lay ignored on the bed. He flopped open her inner thigh—soft, white and bare. Hot mouth…hot tongue. Her body ached for him. Her nipples hardened. She pulled at the towel but he grabbed at her wrist. Held her in place as he licked right on down.

'Danny, please.'

She jerked her hips wantonly. Desperate for him to fill her. He stopped. Dipped lower. Breathed over her. Hot breath on wet flesh. She bucked again.

'You need to be patient or I'll have to teach you a lesson.'

She lay back like a good girl. She thought she might die of need, waiting for his touch, his tongue. Her legs lay open. The towel was still in place, resting above the

V of her thighs—she was exposed to the air and to his heavy, sultry stare.

'Are you going to be more obedient, Georgia?'

Her eyes flew open. She was loving the thrill of his words.

'Yes. *Please.*'

'Because every time you show me disrespect I will have to make you lie back like this—with your legs open wide—and wait for me.'

She felt the stirrings of an orgasm just at his words. She looked down over his torso, over the swells and ridges of hard muscle outlined so clearly.

'Danny, please...*please.* I'll do whatever you want. I need to feel you inside me.'

'Ah, but there you are—impatient. *Again.*'

She saw he wasn't in complete control after all. His neck was strained. She sat up and opened her mouth for him. But he shoved her down. Ripped the towel away.

His eyes widened. Then he bent his head and licked her swollen bud with fierce, unforgiving strokes—once, twice, three times—and she screamed. She screamed and exploded and jerked as he pinned her down. Licked at her until she could take no more.

He wrapped her up in her gown and she yielded softly. Lifted her up into his arms and carried her to a daybed, where he sat with her, holding her, absorbing the after-waves of her pleasure. He'd never taken such joy from a lover's climax before. And he'd never been as completely selfless. But he was relishing every melted moment she lay in his arms.

He heard her mumble something. Stroked her head where it lay against his chest. Shushed her.

He looked around at the spa, at the candles that floated

on the sunken pool, at the clusters of palms, fronds that seemed to wave blessings at their silent, secret moment. *Overwhelming.* His senses were all working in unison and he'd never, ever felt so in tune with himself or another person.

She tilted her face to look up at him. Her eyes were treacle-dark, with only rings of jade visible.

'Your climax is beautiful to watch, Georgia. You open like a flower.'

And she had—it had been as if every part of her had uncurled and shone in the intense light of his touch.

'I've never let anyone do that to me before,' she whispered.

That just made it all the sweeter.

'I've never felt so relaxed, so much trust.'

He smiled at her. She smiled at him. He loved that smile—that mouth that was almost too big for her face. It made everything seem—*right*. He leaned down to kiss her. Just once.

'Shall we get our handmaidens back in? Do you want anything else?'

'I don't think I can move.' Her voice was loose and gravelly.

'Sure you can.' He shifted beside her.

They sat up on the bed, limbs stretched out.

'We could have a dip in that pool.' The one with steps that opened out into a rocky grotto, shielded on all sides and open to the clear sky. 'We could lounge in there all alone.'

He tilted her chin with his finger, dipped his mouth for another of her hot, sweet kisses.

'I didn't bring any swimwear.'

'You're not going to need it.'

He unbelted her robe and held it as she stood up and

stepped out of it. She walked away and he marvelled at the lines of her body as she moved. Pale, slim and strong. She turned her head to see if he was following. Alluring. And oh, so, *so* sexy.

He got up and stepped out with her, loving the lapping of the warm water on his skin. He dived under, needing to feel his muscles work, surfaced and hauled himself out onto the shaded pool-edge, where she sat like a mermaid—naked and natural.

'Not sunbathing?'

She shook her head. 'No, not my thing. I need to keep out of the sun,' she said. 'I'm terrified of sun damage. It runs in my family. One of the reasons why Dubai and I are not suited.'

He felt a faint tang of irritation. Dubai could be whatever you wanted it to be. And if what you wanted wasn't there it soon would be—that was its unique selling point.

'If you're careful you can live out here without anything like that affecting you. And with the life we can have it's got to be worth it.'

She sighed. He looked at her sharply.

'To be honest, for me there's loads to love—but loads I prefer back home. It just feels slightly unreal and *dreamy*. And all the money—and the *stuff*! Everyone is so motivated by *stuff*!'

'Maybe some are—but most of the ex-pats I've met are just happy to be able to have a nice life. Most people respond to reward—and the rewards here are whatever you make them. That's why I love it so much. No ceilings on success. It's all down to you and what you bring to the party. What you make of yourself—not where you come from. It doesn't all begin and end with what your name is.'

Thank God. Because the name Ryan had been like

a set of handcuffs until he'd made his way to London and then here. Over here nobody knew him. Perfect. No name...no pack drill.

'Yet for me who I am *is* where I come from. My little corner of London and my sister are like twin anchors. It's taken me so long to adjust to being without them. And I still feel as if I'm floating away when I'm not there.'

'Does that mean you're going to stay in London, no matter what?'

He couldn't think of anything worse than being tied to his home. He'd suffocate. It would be like being buried alive.

She shook her head. 'Oh, I don't know. I gave it a go— out here—and it didn't work out. I just want to crawl back under my rock for a little while.'

'I can't imagine a bigger travesty than you being hidden away under a rock.' He trailed his broad brown hand down her arm, white-hot. 'You're too beautiful. You should be on display. In a glass case.'

She laughed. 'Palest Woman in the Middle East? That would gather a crowd.'

'Ah, maybe not such a good idea.' He kissed the bare skin of her shoulder, felt the trace of oil transfer to his lips. Went back for more. 'You've kept your skin perfect. Not a trace of even a sun spot.'

'Can't risk it—I've been warned I might get melanomas. My mum...' Her voice trailed away. Then, 'She was my colouring—Babs isn't. Babs is dark. Mum went to Australia when she left school. She didn't think she needed to cover up. Came back and it was too late.'

She twirled her toes in the water, lost in her silence.

'That's tough.' But it explained a lot.

She sent him a quick smile and shrugged.

'So Babs drilled it into me—and we could never afford hot foreign holidays anyway. I think we had a couple of day-trips to France. But mostly she had to work, and I was quite happy to help out. In fact I loved it.'

'Yeah? What could you do in a pub—as a child, I mean?'

'Oh, tons of stuff. Mostly cleaning—which I hated. Helping in the kitchen with the lunches. And serving them. But never behind the bar. Babs was strict about that. Not until I was eighteen.'

She twirled her foot round and round in the water again. Smiled to herself.

He put his arm round her shoulders. Skin on skin. It felt natural. Good.

'We were so close. Just the two of us. And she was so happy for me to get my "lucky break", as she called it—the chance to move away and get a better life. Only I don't see it like that now. Being here has made me realise how much I value my home...London...and—oh, you know—the buzz! The rain...the seasons... Christmas in the cold instead of in sand and sunshine.'

He really didn't know why but he felt even more aggravated by that comment. 'You mean you wouldn't even think about staying out here?' Why was he asking that? What did *he* care?

'I don't have anything to hold me here.'

Her foot stilled in the pool. Ripples spread. Silence lengthened.

'No, I suppose not.'

He still held her, but the easiness of it had gone. Her shoulders were rigid where they lay under his arm. He eased away from her and sank back into the water.

'Swim?'

She smiled a soft little smile. Shook her head.

'I think I'd better go inside now. Just in case. You know...sunburn.'

'Okay. I'll catch you up. Then I need to make some last-minute checks on things—just a few emails.' He braced his hands on the rocky ledge, watching as she stood. A definite detachment. Eve after the apple. 'Will you be ready for eight?'

''Course.'

He watched her walk back inside. No coy over-the-shoulder glance this time. Brisk. Grabbed the robe. Gone.

Every step was a stomp.

She stomped from the spa to the changing room. She grabbed her clothes and stomped along the polished floors to Reception and on to the Honeymoon Suite. She flung open the door and stomped to the bar. Cracked open some water and drank from the bottle—no one to see her; she didn't care.

She'd phone Babs. She'd tell her what she'd done— what she was doing. She'd get a dose of cockney common sense and then she'd feel better. Because, really, what she'd been doing up until now—living in a land of make-believe—*that* was all going to come crashing round her ears any day now. And she really, *really* needed to prepare herself.

She belted the robe tighter, almost satisfied by the uncomfortable tug on her waist. Reached for her phone, where it lay charging on a side table under the shelter of a large-brimmed lamp.

The screen was a blur of messages. She scrolled through them. Shook her head at her own selfishness. She hadn't warned Babs and now the whole world knew what she'd done.

She cringed as she dialled the number—didn't even want to read the messages.

'Georgia, where *are* you? What's happened?'

Her voice was so close she could be standing in The Tavern right now.

'I'm sorry—I got married,' she blurted.

'You got *married*? So it's true? Congratulations! I mean, I didn't believe it at first, but… Wow, sweetheart, who is it?'

How typical of her sister not to give her any guilt—just to sound happy for her. She felt even worse.

'It's a long story, Babs. And I'm sorry I didn't tell you before it—happened.'

'That's not important! It's you that's important—and your husband. Oh, my goodness, Georgia, he looks so handsome in those pictures. Tell me about him.'

'He's…just a guy I met.'

That wasn't the right thing to say. What *was* the right thing to say? She didn't want to tell her the truth. And she didn't want to lie.

'He's lovely, Babs. Kind, generous. Warm, funny. Clever—really, really clever. And, yes…' She sighed, hearing herself. 'He is incredibly handsome.'

'And you love him? More important than any of that. You do love him?'

She swallowed the huge hot bubble in her throat. 'Yes, I love him very much.'

She could almost hear the sigh that Babs exhaled. Could almost see her shoulders sag in satisfaction.

'Thank goodness. That's the main thing. You know, I never, ever thought I would say this, but I always suspected that your wanting to marry Nick was more about filling up an emptiness inside than because you really loved him. But this must be different—you wouldn't have rushed ahead if you weren't sure.'

Oh, she was sure, all right. Sure that she was in deep. And sure that if she didn't put the brakes on immediately she was going to wind up in a giant pile-up of heartache bigger than she had ever thought possible.

'So, do you think you might manage to come home at some point?'

She closed her eyes on the guilt, the shame. 'Babs, I'm sorry that we just—just went ahead and did it without you there. And I promise I'll be home soon—really soon. Honest.'

'Oh, Georgia, that's great. I can't wait to meet him. And to give you my blessing. And don't even *think* about being sorry. I can only imagine how you must have been swept off your feet. A real fairytale wedding.'

And the 'fairytale' would continue with this intimate dinner party later.

She clicked off the phone, never so grateful to end a conversation with her sister in her life. She only hoped she'd figure out what to tell her by the time she finally got home. Because she doubted Babs would be pleased that she'd married a man for money. Even if some of it *was* to pay off her debts.

Indigo was exquisite. Eight courses of the most tiny, delicious morsels she'd ever tasted, matched with perfectly complementary wines. Danny's friends were lovely too, and Georgia was pleased to see that Ursula and her husband were among them.

She wore the colours of the coral reef—bright peaches and dark aquamarines in a simple silk shift. She tied her hair in a messy knot, daubed her lids with turquoise and kept her lips nude. Added nude heels and clutch and a simple turquoise cuff. Her rings sparkled. Her smile sparkled. Her heart was heavy.

Danny was clean-shaven in an exquisitely tailored suit. Bond-like. Lethal.

She had armed herself as best she could. The hours waiting for him to return to the suite had been a blessing. She had slept a little, answered a few texts and emails, read a little. She'd drunk water and filed her nails. A manicurist was on hand, of course, but she would rather maintain some shard of herself in this whirlwind week. And she'd already promised herself she could just about manage nails.

Her heart was another matter entirely. She stared at the band of gold that encased her finger like a vice.

'Georgia, would you like to take coffee out on the terrace?'

She looked up. Danny was watching her. They all were.

'Sorry—I was…'

'You were staring at your beautiful rings and imagining all the wonderful years ahead. Isn't that right, Georgia?'

No wonder Ursula was an ambassador. She'd found the perfect thing to say in a moment when everyone must have been wondering what on earth was wrong with her.

She smiled as broadly as she could. Danny took her hand and squeezed it. She opened her mouth to reply but the words wouldn't come. How could she sit there and lie? She looked at their faces. Expectant, happy faces. Then, as the silence extended, curious.

'Georgia, you'll outshine that diamond every day of your life.'

His friends smiled, happy that the pause had been

filled with such a romantic sentence. She smiled too. What a lovely thing for her new husband to say.

He had been expertly seguing all night. From the *So, how did you two meet?* to the *So, there really is such a thing as love at first sight!* he had skilfully overtaken every answer and switched lane seamlessly into a new subject. Thank goodness—because though they had practised their story—*met at a party, whirlwind romance*—she was such a useless liar that the fewer times she had to talk about it, the better.

They moved to the terrace. To the heavy air that would play havoc with her hair. But still it was easier than sitting in the perfectly chilled dining area under such affectionate scrutiny. She felt Danny behind her, all at once soothing and startling.

He leaned into her, his breath on her ear.

'You've won them over. They love you.' He squeezed her shoulders, placed a kiss on her neck. 'There's not long to go now. There are some photographers outside, apparently. We'll give them a picture on our way out. You all right with that?'

She nodded. The conspiracy continued.

'Great. We'll have one drink—then head back.'

He took her hand, fell into his role beautifully.

They sat out, sipping and chatting and idling away the minutes. He lavished her with attention and affection and her fairytale world seemed woozily real again. The beautiful surroundings, the adorable people, the gorgeous husband, the carefree life. She felt herself teetering on the edge of that seductive, shimmering world. As if she really could slip inside and live it.

The handsome Prince sat on a low chair, legs easy, whisky tumbler dangling in his fingers. Even off duty, even on his *wedding night,* the embers of his power glowed dully. He was magnetic. Everyone was drawn to him and even she found it hard not to bask in his glow.

Man-chat flowed on one side, woman-chat on the other. She half listened, half replied. Danny switched his glass into his other hand and sought out hers. His eyes never moved but the squeeze was one of...*solidarity?...affection?...intimacy?* Whatever it was, it conveyed a little shot of warmth that she drank up greedily.

'So, Danny, you'll have put your brother totally in the shade now.'

His hand tensed. She swivelled her neck to see why. Such a simple sentence from Ursula's husband, Ciaran, but he looked nonplussed. No tense jaw, no frowning eyes. But there had been a definite flare of tension—she'd felt it.

'The first Ryan to be married! You'll be heading home to celebrate? Show off your new bride? Show your brother and sister what they need to do to measure up?'

'Yes, we've got plans to do that. After London. Georgia's sister is first on the list. But all of that comes after the Sheikh. We've got a few days at the palace to get this deal closed down. Georgia's really looking forward to meeting him.'

'Well, you've set the bar for your brother—that's for sure. I'm thinking Mark must be next up. Surely he's going to make an honest woman of that girl?'

'Not sure who he's with at the moment. Georgia—another drink? Or have you had enough?'

'Ah, well, interesting times in the Ryan household. Must admit I never thought that out of the three of you you would be the first to tie the knot. Or to own a company that's about to hit the Fortune Five Hundred list. That must go some way to mending your mother's broken heart.'

'Yeah, well, you shouldn't always judge on appearances. Georgia—let's get out of here, shall we?'

For a moment she just stared. It was the growl in his voice as much as the fluid move out of his seat that startled her.

''Course!'

She stood up—jerked up. Turned to the lovely Ursula and hugged her. The rest of the party fell back into happy chatter, but there was no mistaking the uncomfortable pause

'Have a lovely evening, Georgia, and don't mind his moods. They're much better than they were.' Ursula squeezed her close and smiled. 'And I'm sure we'll become firm friends—call me when you're back from your travels and we'll meet up. Promise?'

Georgia looked round. Danny was saying a swift goodbye with a wave of his hand and a purposeful stride towards the door.

'What just happened there? What's the story with his brother?' she asked Ursula.

'Oh, it's all in the past. Don't worry—I'm sure he'll tell you in his own time.'

Another hug. Another squeeze. Another question raised.

She swallowed. Looked round at this handsome man, with the world at his feet and a dark secret in his heart. She was getting in too deep. Caring too much.

The impulse to cut and run suddenly reared up inside her. She had one million in the bank. She'd seen the bank draft. She'd agreed to stay—to help him play out his charade—but the flames of trouble were crackling more loudly. Should she stay for the other million? Help him to get his longed-for deal?

But what price did she place on her heart?

CHAPTER SIX

'Do not question me. It's not your business.'

Georgia closed her mouth, swallowed. Stunned, almost, by the ferocity of his tone. He thrummed with black anger and she found herself backing away to the far side of the wide leather seat in the chauffeur-driven car.

She had been about to ask—it was true. In the way she would have asked a toddler why he was crying. Because seeing another human in pain hurt her and she wanted to help fix things. His reaction was like that of a damaged child. She had seen it often enough in the inner city nursery where she'd worked before she'd come here. Poor little souls who were angry at the world and didn't know why.

But he was a grown man. A man who commanded, controlled and conveyed power. She'd seen with her own eyes how people deferred to him. And it wasn't through fear: it was through respect. So just what *were* these black moods Ursula referred to? What was the family secret of his mother's broken heart? And could she follow her own advice and stop worrying about it?

The car rolled along through the night. Swollen silence thick with secrets filled the space. Everything outside became so much more interesting than anything inside.

It was like waiting for thunder and the onslaught of torrential rain.

'I'm not going to ask about it…' She began slowly, chose her words carefully. 'But I *am* going to insist that you don't embarrass me like that again. Even for the short time that we'll be together.'

As if a fire had suddenly been ignited the air was devoured. Her breath hitched in her throat as she turned her head to face him. The black mask of his anger darkened—then dropped.

'Apologies.'

'You've said that to me before. But it's just a word. Like when you apologised for Tommy, or whatever his name was, for being lewd in the elevator. Just words.'

He raged. She could see it in his face, feel it in his presence. A symphony of *sturm und drang*. Black, dark and unforgiving. She could sense his battle to regain control. She could see it too. His fingers had curled into fists and his clean-shaven jaw was square and tense.

'It's not just a word, Georgia.'

His voice was a curl of control. A quiet, low growl. He was fearsome.

But she was not afraid. Emotions didn't faze her. Losing her job, letting her sister down, never getting home—those things were worth worrying about. Anger was an emotion. She could handle that. And she could handle *him*. He might have the rest of the world cowering when things weren't just the way he wanted, but not her. For some reason she felt that she understood him, that she could see past his fury.

Her problem wasn't that he made her fearful. Her problem was all the other emotions he'd unleashed.

'It is until you act it out. Danny, whether or not I was acting as your wife, tonight I was your guest. And I—

and everybody else in our company—deserved to be treated well.'

'They were treated perfectly well,' he growled. 'That's the best restaurant in the Emirates. We had everything we could possibly want there—the view, the food, wine, service…'

'Yes. And we had *you*. The best possible host. The man everybody defers to. The one everyone wanted to be with tonight. Everybody looks up to you.'

She couldn't see his face at all now. But it was clear she had his attention.

'But no one wants to be in the middle of something like that! We were having a lovely time until you got angry—and I don't want to know the reason. I just want you to appreciate the reaction—of everybody. That's all.'

She waited for him to interject but his blank face had been turned away from her.

'The world seems to revolve around you, Danny. The sun, moon and stars are all just waiting for your bidding. But the moment things aren't exactly as you've planned them this horrible…*darkness* falls. It's like a black hole. And we all get sucked inside until you decide that the sun can come out again.'

The intensity of his presence was almost stifling, but it had to be said. She couldn't just pretend that it was all right.

'I'm sorry if you don't want to hear it, Danny, but if I didn't care then I wouldn't bother saying anything…'

'What do you mean *care*?' Words were fired out like thunderclaps. 'Care isn't part of the deal, Georgia. You're not sitting in the back of my car because we *care* about each other. You're here because you've entered into a business deal. There's no place for emotions here.'

In the pause that followed they stared at each other.

'Sorry. I'm sorry. That was an appalling thing to say.'

'No, you're quite right,' she managed to reply. 'You're absolutely right. But you're letting yourself be crucified by anger. And *that's* emotion, Danny. Whether you recognise it or not. And being like that is not going to help you, your business, or anyone else around you—whether they *care* about you or not.'

The words said, she sat back. If she could have got out right there on the road she would have. But she was in the middle of a scene that she'd signed up to, as well as in the middle of a six-lane highway in a luxury car, with a luxury man who, despite what he said, had more emotions running through him than a river in torrent.

His words had been well timed. Just when she'd begun to fear that she might actually fall for him!

There was no doubt that she was vulnerable just now. She'd barely shed a tear after Nick. And even realising that she'd be stuck here working for the next two years at least hadn't really upset her at the time—she'd just got on with it. But *this*?

This past twenty-four hours had sent her into an emotional vortex in which everything was spinning, dredging up feelings she hadn't even known she had. Loneliness, self-pity, and—more worryingly—this strange vulnerability she was developing with a man who could hurt her more with his words than Nick had with a broken engagement.

'I said I was sorry and I meant it. I don't expect you to understand what happened back there and I—I can't go into it just now. But I *am* sorry. I don't want to hurt you and I do appreciate that you care. I really do.'

He tried to reach across for her hand. She really didn't deserve to be treated as anything other than precious and he'd totally screwed this up. Sure, this deal was time-limited, but being with her was great—the best. He closed his fingers round her hand, felt the sharp ridges of her engagement ring dig into his palm. He turned her hand round, looked at it. Tilted it to catch the streetlights as they passed. Tried to understand the crazy mess his head was in right now.

The car rolled to a halt. She tugged her hand free, grabbed up her bag and got out without waiting for the valet to open the door.

Damn this situation. Damn that comment by Ciaran.

Maybe he hadn't meant it. And heaven knew why it should still be raw—but, hey… At least there was *some* progress. The words had still burned. But much less than they had before. Ten years ago if anyone had said anything about Mark and Maya he would have thrown a punch. At least now he could just seethe and leave.

Progress, he thought bitterly. Little by little. His therapist would be so proud.

He exited the car and walked behind Georgia. Her pride was magnificent to watch. Everything about her was self-contained. It came naturally to her, but manufacturing his own self-containment had taken years.

'Georgia—wait.'

She was striding away. Out through the lobby and into the courtyard garden. Another couple sat deep in the shade of a tropical pergola but he barely registered anything except the tilt of her head and the stretch of her shoulders.

'Please, Georgia—wait.'

She quickened her pace. He lengthened his stride. Caught her wrist and pulled her back. She turned her face away—towards the ocean, away from his touch. He clasped her arms. Still her face was turned. He cupped her chin, swivelled it. Soft, beautiful cheeks streaked with tears. Caused by him.

It was like a sucker punch to his stomach. He felt worse than ever. What had he done?

He grabbed her in close. Held her rigid body against him. Felt the moisture of her tears soak his shirt. But she was firm as white marble. Unflinching.

'I'd really like to get some rest now.' She spoke to the rolling waves, to the vast empty sky. 'If you really need me to come to the Sheikh's palace then I will.'

His mind whirred. She was actually thinking about walking out now? He felt that sensation again—not anger...but what?

'I want you to come. I've told him all about you. He's expecting you.'

'Then I'll come. I'll not let you down.'

Weariness sighed through her, making him even more alert.

'Okay.'

She *had* to come. He'd planned all this in his head now—worked out all the angles. got the story watertight. And, damn it all, he was enjoying being with her.

Having to get married to keep this project on course had been the biggest gamble he'd ever taken, but it seemed it was all working out perfectly. And he could keep a lid on his anger—he'd show her that. Until this weekend it had been months, *years* since he'd lost control like that.

She pulled out of his arms. 'I need to sleep now. It's been a long day.'

He let her slide out of his grasp but held on to her hand, walked by her side to their suite. Maybe from a distance they looked like a honeymoon couple. They looked good together. He liked the way she suited him. Liked her long-legged stride, her straight-spined hauteur. Head up, shoulders back—she took on the world.

But her stride tonight did not have the confident cut that had so struck him at the Al-Jafar. Tonight—her wedding night—she was walking as if to face some dreaded news.

He should be pausing now, spinning her in his arms, tilting her back. She should be laughing up into his face, her eyes dancing with the promise of what was about to happen. And then he should be scooping her up as she threw back her head, locked her arms round his neck and slid into his embrace with love in her heart and desire in her blood.

Not quite.

They stopped at the threshold. She looked away. He fumbled with the door. Eventually it swung open. The staff had been in, of course. It was like a fairyland. Little candles flickered like fireflies, floating in all corners of the room. The huge white bed, veiled from the ceiling, was covered in flowers and scents. Petals on the sheets.

That was all he noticed—he didn't want to see any more. He swallowed. For once in his life words stuck in his throat like unswung punches.

'You'll have the bed, of course.'

She slanted a look at him, avoiding his eyes. 'Of course.'

She moved away, this beautiful woman who'd fallen into his path, who'd rightly or wrongly become his wife for the week. He'd given her the best terms he could because she was trading something that she valued so highly. And it was all in the name of the deal. *Everything* was in pursuit of the deal.

He must not lose his focus on that now. It was crucial that he closed this. So much was riding on it. *Huge.*

It was huge. His pride, his reputation and his word. His stocks and shares and his CEO profile. And politically, morally, it meant the betterment of conditions for thousands of immigrant workers.

And the true glittering prize would be the satisfaction of knowing he'd done it all by himself. No other Ryan at his back. Not a whiff of the nepotism he so despised.

She was running. Fleeing. Through the park, past the pond. She could see her friends on swings, flying high in the air. They couldn't help her. She could hear the horrible words like spears in her back: 'Little orphan Annie, hasn't got a daddy.' Sing-song and nasty.

She could see the roofline of The Tavern, getting closer and closer. But there was no doorway. Just windows—people inside smiling, Babs pulling pints of frothy beer, passing them across the bar. She rattled the windows—no one could hear her. She went round and round the building to find the door and the words rained down on her back. Mocking, laughing. Sharper than blows.

Georgia sat up. Dark. Hot. A sheen of sweat between her breasts. That dream. She hadn't had that dream since she was a child. She panted. Slowly stilled her breathing. How strange.

It had been so vivid. It had been common back then, and she would wake screaming and run to Babs, climb in beside her and snuggle under her arm as her big sister soothed her better.

'Don't worry about what they say. They don't have what we have, Georgia,' she would say. 'We've got each other and no one's love is stronger.'

If the cuddles didn't work Babs would warm some milk and dollop in honey, choose a fairy story from the shelf and read to her about princesses in faraway lands where handsome princes would cut through forests and kill wild beasts to save them. And then she'd drift off to sleep, dreaming that one day her very own handsome prince would be there to rescue her.

Light. A phone screen suddenly illuminated.

The rest of the room was dark, but for the satiny sheets and the tumble of rose petals that spilled from the bed to the floor.

Danny. She could sense him. Even in sleep the low glow radiated. She got out of bed and padded over. Lifted the phone—Danny's phone. A message from his sister Frankie.

Mum's desperate to see you. And Georgia ;-) She must be some girl to put up with you. Mark sends his best, as ever. Take care x

She put the phone down. Hadn't really meant to read the message. She wasn't a snooper but she did care for him—no matter how hard he tried to fend her off. He was afflicted by something from his past. Something had driven him out and was still driving him on. The relentlessness was almost palpable.

Of course he wouldn't thank her for caring. Not at all. But she couldn't help herself. She was a nurturer by nature—always wanting to fix things, to make things better.

That was another of the reasons why she longed to get back to London and all its bleak bustle. Her East End kids had none of the advantages of the children of diplomats and industrialists. East End kids needed to know that they could dream and they could achieve. She loved watching them grow and develop. It was so fulfilling. Her Dubai international children were lovely too—of course they were—but they had so much already, and parents who would do anything for them—anything money could buy, that was.

Not for the first time she wondered about Danny's mother. She must miss him terribly. And, whatever it was that had broken her heart, to be deprived of her son...so far away and still hurting so much...must make it almost impossible to mend.

The phone's screen faded. There was the low thrum of air-conditioning. Breathing.

Her eyes adjusted to the gloom and she saw his outline, lying by the sofa, on the floor. She walked closer. He was face-down, the line of his back and his legs just visible, like a streak of gold. His head was on bent arms, cradling a cushion. His breathing was deep and even. He was so, so perfect in slumber. She felt the urge to lie down beside him, touch him, inhale him, get lost in him...

Their lives had collided for now. Just for this week. Soon they would be in their separate domains again. She back in London with Babs and he here—king of his corporation, issuing his orders and building more and more of his empire.

What she was going to be able to do for Babs was priceless, though. To lift her from the misery of all that debt and offer her the chance to retire, if that was what she wanted. She could sell the pub—maybe buy a house in the country. Georgia could go and stay with her at weekends. It didn't matter—they'd have plenty of time to plan it all out when she got back. It would be amazing. She should be looking forward to it!

And she would—she really would—as soon as the Sheikh's deal was signed. As soon as Danny left her in London.

'Are you all right?'

Startled, she put her hand out to grip the back of the
sofa. His voice was gravelly from sleep. He turned.
Rested on one elbow.

'Yes. Your phone went off—a message from Frankie.'

She passed it to him and watched the sleep-softened
lines of his face light up as he read it. His eyebrows rose
slightly, but that was all he gave away.

'Would you like to sleep on the bed? I hate to see you
on the floor. It's not comfortable.'

He smiled a little at that, clicked off his phone, looked
at her.

'Kind of you, but I'm fine—I could sleep on the edge
of a knife.'

'I'm sure you could—there doesn't seem to be anything you *can't* do—but, honestly, the bed's huge. You
should get a good sleep before tomorrow.'

He sat right up. The dawn light was filtering in and
it washed him in more gold. He rested his elbows on his
knees and cocked his head. Was it possible there was a
sexier man on this earth? She didn't think so.

'Georgia, if you invite me into that bed there is no
chance in hell that I'll be able to keep my hands off you—
you know that, right?'

'I...I honestly wasn't thinking that.'

It sounded like a lie. But she truly hadn't meant to invite him to sleep with her. Distance—it was all about distance. She'd had some fun with him and look where *that*
had got her. The bruises that she'd thought had cleared
from her heart had bloomed again. And she knew without question that it would be much more than sorrow
she would feel if she let herself get any more involved
with him.

She also knew that even having this short time with
him had wasted her for any other man to come after. Who

was going to measure up? The only thing—the only im-perfection—was his dark anger, and even that drew her like a moth to a flame. She wanted to help him past it. Yes, she was on a very choppy sea in a very tiny life raft.

So sharing a bed…

'You're right. It wouldn't be a good idea.'

He laughed. 'I didn't say that. In fact I think it would be a great idea. And we're going to have to work out a game plan for the Sheikh. I don't imagine he will think that us newlyweds will want twin beds.'

'No, I suppose not…'

He raised his eyebrows. A chuckle rolled over his face for a moment, then he was serious and solemn. 'No. And that's when it will count.'

He stood up now, gave a fluid, powerful stretch, and walked long-limbed and purposeful to the bar. Naked apart from the tight black boxers that moulded his glutes and drew her hungry gaze. She looked away. He reached into the chiller and took out two bottles of water.

'You awake enough to talk now? It's almost five any-way.'

''Course.' She was awake. And talking was good.

He handed her a glass of water. She sat cross-legged on the bed. He sat opposite her.

'I said it last night but I want to say it again—apolo-gies for my reaction to Ciaran's question. Georgia, I have an issue with my brother—Mark. It goes way back. I thought I had completely moved past it, but—well, as you saw last night. it still rankles.'

She nodded, sipped her water, tucked her hair behind her ear, watched him.

'I can't afford to be anything other than in the game when we get to Salim's. So I owe you a bit of back story and then we can prep this—work out the angles and manage any risks. You okay with that?'

'You know I am. I'll do what I can to help—as long as you do what you can to keep calm. Danny, I appreciate everything you've done for me, and I honestly would go with you to Salim's, if it helped, without the extra money. I hope you know that? You've changed my life and Babs's life for ever." More than he would ever know.

He nodded, took a swift swig of water. 'Good. Thanks. But you're doing me a favour too, remember? Salim might have backed off the whole deal if he felt I wasn't the type of guy he wanted to associate with. And, yeah, there's no doubt that emotions *have* surfaced in me with you being around. But you're not the cause—*I* am the cause, Georgia. I might not have completely mastered them, but that's nothing to do with anyone other than me.'

He reached across for her hand, squeezed it, smiled. Squeezed her heart too.

'So…the Sheikh.'

'The Sheikh?' she repeated.

He raised his eyebrow and the serious cast of his face slipped into place. The soft lilt was sharpened. 'I've been courting this deal for years. Three, to be exact. And even before that, I suppose, in terms of building links to get close to him. This project is to build state-of-the-art sport and leisure facilities—stadiums, arenas, indoor lakes… you name it. There will be international events located there and we want to be ahead of the madness when the contracts are awarded.'

'Wow—sounds ambitious, even for Dubai.'

He shrugged. 'Yes, but it's completely doable, and when the construction starts I want there to be more beneficiaries than just the fat cats.'

'Meaning?'

'Manual workers. Immigrants. You know how badly they can be treated out here, Georgia—and that doesn't sit well with me. Never has. I can't stand those who bleed others dry to get a few extra bucks.'

She knew what he meant. Even in her complex there were stories of how badly some of the house staff had been treated before the company she worked for had taken it over. And that Danny cared enough to factor this in was no surprise. One more good quality in amongst the others.

'But even with what I've built up I still need a backer. And Salim is someone I respect. He's more than money. He's principled. He gets it. He knows that Dubai has built up a reputation as well as a tourist industry. And he cares about his culture. It's all about respect. I respect him and I expect the same in return. So in terms of this week he'll appreciate that we are married. It gives me an air of respectability too, Georgia. And, though he may suspect that it's more of a business arrangement than a love-match, it would be good to have a story without holes. There will be less embarrassment that way. For all concerned.'

She nodded. She could do this. If the net result of it was that hundreds of families benefited, then she was totally going to be there for Danny.

'That will require us to act like a newly married couple whilst behaving modestly. Are you going to be able to do that? Without it meaning anything?'

He was focussed on her. Intently. The sharp, intelligent eyes reading her.

She swallowed. 'I know what this is, Danny. And I know what it's not.'

He nodded. 'I think we have to broach this, Georgia. There's no point in glossing over it.' He lifted her hand again. 'I think when we started this it was quite simple. I'm incredibly attracted to you. You're a sharp, beautiful girl. And we cooked up a plan to get us both out of trouble. But things have run away from us a bit. Maybe that was inevitable—but we need to get it back on track before we go.'

'I know. I agree. And it should be simple—shouldn't it? It's not as if we're going to be on each other's continent, never mind in the same social circles, after this week. I think we'll be able to cope.'

She tried to give him a reassuring smile. Tried to reassure herself too. She would miss him—the fast pace, the sensation of being with a human furnace that made things happen, got things done. He was a man of power. And of honour.

'Can we pull it off, Georgia? The physical side? Without getting burned?'

His fingers traced circles in her palm and the sparkle of desire flew straight to her core, lighting a hot path. She stared into those pure blue eyes. *Could* they pull it off? She had no doubt *he* could. But she was under no illusions.

This was going to be a week she would look back upon and wonder at. She'd be able to dine out on the story with her girlfriends. Kirsty and the rest had sent countless messages already, and she'd give them the truth—one day.

'I think we can pull off the physical side very well. I don't think anyone will doubt that we are attracted to each other.'

'Oh, I have no doubt that people will see *exactly* how attracted we are.'

He lifted his hand to her face, trailed his knuckles down her cheek, let his thumb drag across her bottom lip. Lit an instant trail of lust. He leaned forward for a kiss. She felt the full push of his tongue inside her mouth. Zero to incendiary again.

He pushed her down on the bed. Leaned over her. Took his fill of her mouth. Kissed her. Mastered her. The same as before. She allowed him to take and to dominate. And then she gave it back. Directed the kiss to suit her. Suckled his bottom lip, loving the sensual play and the thrill of tasting and touching. He let her take what she wanted. She moaned her pleasure. He swallowed it and breathed his own right back. They were so perfectly matched. It was so easy to give in because everything was so—*right*.

As long as she didn't give too much. As long as she held something back. Losing herself in him, surrendering—the temptation was immense. But she mustn't.

She pulled away, breathless. Turned her face to the side to say what was etched in her heart, scared that if she didn't say it now she might never say it. And he had to know—she had to keep him onside to help her get through these days intact.

'I can only do this if we don't take it any further than we already have. I'm being honest with you, Danny. I've already done things—felt things—that I never imagined doing or feeling before. And if we… If I sleep with you I think I might lose a bit of myself. For ever.'

He leaned back immediately. Straight arms. Reared himself up. 'Georgia, I appreciate your honesty.'

She kept her head twisted away. Stared at the sofa, the candles, the bottles of water on the bar. Stared at the daybreak stealing in through the white-veiled French doors, seeping onto the dark wooden floor, beginning one more day for her as Mrs Ryan. She stared at the honeymoon suite and imprinted its details on her mind.

She felt him shift his weight away from her on the bed. She'd panicked him?

But he sat beside her, lifted her hand to pull her up. Cuddled her under the strength of his arm. Pressed her head to his chest and smoothed down her hair.

'There's no point in pretending, Georgia. If you were going to stay on here in Dubai maybe we could see where it went—but even then it would be hard, you know… Married in the eyes of the world but really just getting to know one another. I don't know…'

He rocked her a little, held her while she let those words fall into place. She imagined for a moment that she might stay on in this oven of a city. She wouldn't need to work as much—could stop the coaching and the extra tutoring. Could slip back into the life she'd enjoyed for a while with Nick, where every day had been sugar-coated and the future had sparkled temptingly.

But was that really who she was? Would she feel fulfilled teaching the privileged as opposed to those to whom she could really make a difference? And, anyway, it would only last as long as Danny was interested in her. Because even with more money, and being able to hang out with her friends, life in Dubai would be dry and barren and arid without his heat and light. And worse would be watching him move on with his life when they crashed and burned.

No, she could not frame that in her head. Better to cut her ties, resign from her job and start over back in the UK.

'I'm not staying, Danny. There's too much waiting for me back in London. My sister, my old job—being able to go from the house to the car to the shops without burning or freezing to death in air-conditioning. And not having to worry every day about my skin.'

'I can't offer you anything more than this week, Georgia.'

It was as if he hadn't heard her.

'I can't promise that we could ever make a go of things. But I *am* sure that we will never forget this time together. And I genuinely think we'll stay friends after this. I don't…I can't actually imagine not having you in my life in some way.'

Like a dip in the pool on a hot afternoon…like fire-side warmth on a cold, damp day…she let his words wrap around her. Absorbed for a moment what he'd said. And then dismissed it.

He'd be so wrapped up in reaching his next milestone there'd be no way he'd have the time, never mind the in-clination, to keep in touch. He hardly saw his family—how would he find time to meet up with a girl? A friend? But she wasn't going to blow holes in that particular state-ment right now. That would take care of itself in time.

'That's a lovely thing to say, Danny. And I would like it to be true. So, yes, let's leave it at that. And I really appreciate you understanding my position and not pres-suring me. Thanks.'

'Georgia, the very last thing I would ever want to do is put you under any pressure. You've already gone above and beyond in agreeing to help me out like this. My sis-ter's right—she usually is, to be fair—but she nailed it when she said you must be some girl. You are. And you can trust me to pull back now, keep things professional—how about that?'

He chuckled as he said it, his laughter lines crinkling and that sensational smile brightening his face. He was right back in the game.

'I've been in training for this business meeting for months. I can feel the adrenalin—it's like pre-match nerves. I feel wired.'

He stood up. Put out his hand for hers. Pulled her to her feet.

'Come on, partner—let's get some breakfast and start to bring this home.'

CHAPTER SEVEN

SLOE-EYED AND DOE-EYED. The salon Georgia was seated in was overflowing with Arabian beauties. Sisters, cousins and wives of Salim and his brothers. Dressed in an array of stunning clothes, bare-headed and beautiful.

Gilded chaises, Arabic mosaic floors and Islamic ceilings—the palace was the last word in luxury. Plates of dates and *petits fours* that nobody touched. Polite, intelligent charming conversation from the senior members of the family. Itchy, impatient whining from the littlest— the ones with whom she had most sympathy. It was all she could do not to drop onto the floor beside them and start to play clapping games.

The men, of course, were in another room. Just as Danny had described. He'd been at pains—in fact he'd almost *been* a pain—to describe what he thought would happen and make sure she was not going to be caught out.

They would be separated almost immediately. He would be taken off for a polite reception and then straight on to business talks with the back-up of his legal team, who were travelling separately. Georgia would be entertained by the women and then pampered to within an inch of her life before they all got together again. Then there would be two separate parties tonight, with the men finally joining the women towards the end of the night.

Their story was simple, and as close to the truth as they could make it. They'd met at a party—true. It had been in one of Dubai's international hotels—also true. They'd lost touch and then been reintroduced and the rest was extremely public history.

Wasn't it just?

Danny had been relentless about drilling into her new information about his business—large, multi-national engineering—his background—the Sheikh loved horse racing too—his UAE habits—eighteen-hour days, the occasional game of rugby...yes, that *was* how he'd got the bump on his nose...and most surprisingly his Canteen Charity project.

He'd brushed over that quickly but she'd paused and looked right at him as they'd sat together on his jet for their tiny flight into the desert.

'You feed the families of your workforce?'

He'd looked uncomfortable, shrugged. 'Not my workforce—the construction workers. You know how bad the poverty is for some of the immigrants here. We've all got to do our bit. And it keeps me grounded. It's very easy out here to get lost in the luxury.'

She'd looked at him again. More closely. This powerhouse, this driven, intense, testosterone-fuelled man. It really was no surprise that he had a compassionate side too. She'd seen the way his face had softened when he'd spoken about his mother, when he'd read the text from his sister, when he'd realised he'd overstepped the mark with Georgia herself.

And this attention to detail for people close and far away—she could see more and more clearly that he was the consummate risk-manager when it came to business. And, though he'd been furious at getting sold an invitation to a dodgy party, he'd simply focussed on the solution and powered ahead.

It was awe-inspiring how much effort he was putting into pulling this off. He'd covered more angles than the princess cut diamond that flashed on her finger. He'd messaged ahead to say that he would be bringing his new wife with him—omitting, of course, to say just how new she was. But there was no need. Their story had been run in the dailies and on the celebrity news feeds in various parts of the world so it was no secret. And Danny was more and more convinced that they'd done the right thing.

When she'd questioned again whether they'd really had to go through with a ceremony, he'd said, 'Sheikh Salim would have found out in seconds that we weren't properly married. No amount of stories would have prevented rumour and speculation. And business with a tainted business partner would not have been sanctioned at all—no matter what foundations we'd already laid down. It's still a huge gamble but the odds are much better this way. Trust me.'

And she did.

Danny had played his part beautifully and helped her to do the same. From the moment they'd walked down the steps onto the Tarmac at the Sheikh's private airstrip he'd been attentive, polite, charming, respectful and appropriately distant. For that she was grateful. Distance was a commodity she was going to have in spades next week. It would be good to start having a taste of it now.

Energy suddenly filled the room. Men in *dishdashas* swarmed in, calling and chattering. The women seemed delighted. And there stood Danny at the back, looking pleased, relaxed and focussed. His eyes were on her. Only on her.

Salim addressed her. 'My dear, your husband has indeed the strongest work ethic of any of us. Imagine that yesterday was your wedding day—and here you are today, waiting while we conclude our talks. But I have spared you any more waiting. We will leave the legal teams to sort out the details—your wedding must be celebrated!'

Danny made his way over. She felt all eyes on them, but his were like a beacon, calling her home. He was smiling his half-smile. He looked confident. He looked happy. He looked as if the world was at his feet. He lifted her hand to his lips and kissed it lightly, his eyes never leaving hers. She wanted to ask if the deal was done— had he pulled it off? She wanted to cover him in kisses and tell him how wonderful he was.

But they'd agreed on a business partnership. It was all about the show. And now she had to take her cue from him—had to be restrained and reserved. She had to play her part respectfully and cause absolutely no ripples other than ripples of satisfaction for Salim that his guests were acting appropriately, as befit his status.

'Georgia and I are delighted that you have taken such trouble to welcome us and to help us celebrate, Salim. And Georgia is completely part of the plan—she's supported me so well since I've known her and this project means a lot to her too.'

Salim turned. He was a smaller man than Danny, but broader, and his imposing presence was softened by a very down-to-earth openness.

'Yes, I understand sport is a big part of your life too? You coach junior football?'

He began to walk her through the room. She felt Danny slip into place behind them, busy in conversation. A slight feeling of panic fluttered through her. She was so anxious that she didn't let him down. And Salim had done his homework. Clearly…

'Yes, I coach girls and boys from four to eight.' She smiled. 'I know it's a bit unusual. I fell into it by accident when I was volunteering at a local youth club. They needed activities to get young kids hooked into, to stop them prowling the streets—and, believe it or not, I am actually quite good at it.'

'I believe it easily, my dear. And I know of at least one young lady who would love to go to your club, were it close at hand.' He pointed out one of the more boisterous young girls, whose energy and smile were compelling. 'My youngest daughter, Samira. She never sits still and can do amazing things with a ball. Did you play when you were her age?'

They were now on the outdoor walkway that lined one side of this great palace. Marble such as she'd never seen before was laid out in vast strips inlaid with contrasting diagonal patterns. Huge domes gleamed and Arabian archways stretched across a myriad of criss-crossing pathways, broader than ten soccer pitches. Palms in regular dots broke up the lines and sharp angles, the tiers of grass and vast stairways.

It was easily the most spectacular space she had ever seen. Truly palatial and magnificent. She might have been overawed by the ostentatious opulence, but the low, easy tones of Danny behind her soothed her nerves. She could do this. Of course she could.

'I suppose I must have played—I don't really remember.'

'You grew up without a mother and father—is that right? That must have given you a different childhood?'

Slightly startled by the frankness of the question, Georgia faltered for a second. 'Yes, my childhood was definitely different. But it was completely filled with love—and for me, that's the most important thing.'

'Love is always the most important thing,' Salim replied as he walked, and she felt the echo of his words and the dull strike of his heels. 'It soothes so many pains. But it can create its own problems when it is not nurtured and protected.'

She stepped along beside him. Silence fell as she digested his words. Was he implying something about their marriage? Or about her childhood?

'All I know is that children who are loved unconditionally and consistently are those who are better able to take their place in the world.'

The Sheikh paused and the whole troupe that followed also paused. 'And of course that is what you will do—you and Danny—for your own children. If you are blessed as I have been.'

She stared at the sharp dark eyes and felt a hot, painful tug in her chest. To be blessed with children was her silent dream. To give a child the love and family that she and Babs had missed out on. And to share that love with her husband.

A fierce, unbidden image of Danny as a father crashed through her mind, jolting her and winding her. But she was not going to stall—not now.

'I will give all children my love—the ones I teach and, if I am blessed, as you say, the ones I shall mother. But none of us knows the future.'

Salim surveyed her, cast his gaze over her as if measuring her. Then he nodded slightly and turned, restarted on his path.

'You have many good qualities, my dear. I am pleased to see that. I have met others who would talk to me about aesthetics rather than truth. You have depth. And humility.' He turned to give her another scrutinising look. 'I am sure we will get on very well.'

She smiled back as they walked on, their pace matching, and an easiness stole over her shoulders. 'I certainly hope so. I would like that for Danny's sake, if nothing else.'

'You would do a lot for Danny's sake, I think.'

She swallowed her immediate thoughts and let that hang between them. 'Yes—yes, I would do almost anything.'

And she meant it.

She felt fingers lacing through hers. She felt the tug of Danny's hand and the wrap of his body close behind her. She knew better than to expect any more affection than that—both because it was public and impolite and also because she had quite clearly asked him not to. This was now business. Strictly business. And, yes, part of that was pulling off the act, but mostly it was about bringing home the deal.

'Your lovely new wife has got me thinking, Danny.'

Danny caught up with them, kept his fingers laced in hers. 'She has a habit of that, Salim. I think I've spent more time questioning myself since I met her than at any other time in my life.'

Well, she hadn't expected *that*! She turned with a startled gaze and he answered with a flashing grin, the quick squeeze of the hand and a wink.

'So what has she got you thinking? Don't tell me—a Dubai Little League?'

'I could think of worse plans, my friend. But we can hatch them later—let's have some refreshments before we retire to prepare for the banquet.'

An aide appeared. Salim excused himself and went off, trailed by a host of other men. Danny watched them go with a speculative look. 'I hope that doesn't indicate anything. We still haven't signed on the dotted line.'

'But it's gone well? So far, I mean?'

He nodded, still staring after them. 'Yes. He's been particularly careful, though. Asked me more details than even I anticipated. Totally grilled me—every aspect of every angle. Thank God I was prepared. And thankfully my legal team are better than excellent. This has been the toughest deal I've ever negotiated in my life.'

He turned back to look at her, his gaze fierce.

'He's really interested in *you*. He's certainly done his homework, and I think he's possibly on to us, but for him I don't think our motivation's the point. It's respect and honour that are important.'

'And love.'

She said it before she could stop herself. And she felt as if she was in freefall, seeing where the words would land with him.

'I don't mean…you know…that we…'

'I know what you mean. Emirati people place huge emphasis on the family and on close relationships. On love, if that's how you want to frame it. So, yes…' He turned his eyes away, staring out over the vast now empty courtyard, perhaps thinking about Salim, perhaps thinking about his family. Perhaps thinking about her. 'It's all about the relationships.'

He frowned. Then turned back to her as if seeing her for the first time.

He put his hands on her shoulders and stroked down her arms. 'You're doing a great job, Georgia. I couldn't ask for more.'

He looked around them—there was no one to see apart from a solitary man walking purposefully through the huge hot space. His white *dish-dasha* flowed in the sudden breeze that had wafted in from the desert, his dark sandaled feet the only contrast between robes and gleaming marble.

Danny stepped closer, into her space. His eyes dropped to her mouth. Her eyes focussed on his face. Stubble was darkening his skin. His lips were deep as burgundy. And parted. Slightly parted. His white dress shirt was open at the neck and she longed to touch the tip of her tongue to the groove of his collarbone—to lick and to taste. The firm outline called out to be touched.

She felt a softening, a readying, and a heart-deep longing. Just being beside him was intoxicating.

He reached for her and a swift wave of arousal washed through her. He wrapped her up. Hugged her. Held her close to his body and tucked his head on top of hers.

'We're nearly home, Georgia. There's just the banquet and then I'm sure we'll be out of here, with the biggest pay-off imaginable.'

She nodded into his chest as her fingers closed round handfuls of his shirt. She wanted more—so much more—but the firm muscle under the skin against her cheek steadied her like a wall of strength and fortitude. Of *course* he was going to get the biggest pay-off imaginable. He was a winner. A doer. And it lit her up from within just to be with him.

'I'm much more conservative than you, Danny—I can't count my chickens until they've hatched. But I have every faith in you. I can't imagine anyone ever saying no to you.'

He pushed her back with a smile. 'You did. It took all of my powers of persuasion to get you to agree to this. Remember?'

She smiled. Nodded.

He turned her round, took her hand in his and walked them back to join the rest of the party.

'Well, you can't blame me. It did seem like the craziest idea imaginable.'

'Does it still seem so crazy?'

'We're not done yet.'

'There you go again. Keep the faith, Mrs Ryan. It's going to work out.'

'As I said, Mr Ryan, I don't count my chickens until they've hatched.'

Danny waited for her.

The dancers with swords, the dancers with drums, the singing and the yelling and the partying had gone on for hours. It wasn't a wedding, but it was traditional. And he was utterly indebted to Salim for such a wonderful display of hospitality.

The legal teams had worked on into the early evening. Very few details were still left to be ironed out. Salim was happy—that much was clear. But he wanted assurances that the environmental impact assessments would not hold anything up when the work moved forward. This was giving Danny's business consultants a minor headache, trying to amend contracts and seek assurances, but it looked as if those chickens had well and truly hatched, and soon they'd be coming home to roost.

The only minor drawback was the lack of one tall, slim, wide-mouthed redhead.

She was having the time of her life, he'd been reliably informed, partying with the ladies in another room. There were chocolate fountains, sweets, and delicious morsels to eat. The hugest banquet imaginable. And of course she'd spent hours being massaged, primped and preened, her hair and make-up being fixed by Salim's staff.

She and the rest of the girls were dancing the night away and he was missing her. Badly.

Salim had spoken candidly to him. 'A good choice. You are well matched,' he had told him. As if it was an arranged marriage and luckily it had worked out well.

Danny had nodded—what else could he have done? On appearances it *was* great! And there was still some crazy part of him that momentarily believed they were an actual married couple. But that was just ridiculous. They'd got on with this—got on with each other—because they had a clear purpose, a joint mission to take a disaster and turn it into an opportunity. And it had worked like a dream.

But two people who had known each other for less than a week had no chance of sticking a marriage out. Look at where they'd both wound up with their previous partners. People they'd been with for months—in his case years. That loser Nick, her fiancé, who'd dumped her in the middle of town and gone off with some piece of fluff. What a jerk. If he could get his hands on him...

And then, of course, there was Maya. And Mark.

He waited to taste the sourness in his mouth. He checked his hands for the familiar fists that always formed when that particular memory blasted him. But, no. He splayed his fingers on his close-cut black dinner suit trousers. Interesting—that had to mark a watershed moment. It was the first time he could remember not wanting to smash his fist into his brother's ribs for stealing his girl.

He ran the image again. Nope. Nothing.

He stood. He wanted—no, needed—a stroll. Wanted to take the night air in, no matter how hot and humid. Some men were going to go through to the ladies' party soon, and he would be one of them. But first he needed some time to think. He had to get his head straight for the trip home.

Once he and Georgia were on that flight back to the UK he might be wrapped up in the finer details of the deal and getting started on setting things in motion. He would need to clear his head before reuniting with his family. Though he couldn't wait to see Frankie.

She'd been his rock through every drama in his life. Though he had a feeling things were going a bit off-piste for her at the moment. She was being unusually quiet about her partnership with Rocco Hermida, the international polo player, entrepreneur and, as far as Danny could see, all-round idiot. But, God, she was defensive about *him* too.

Anyway—that was her problem, her business. She'd have her nose in and about his as soon as he caught up with her. And if he'd thought he needed to be watertight and shipshape for Salim he was nothing compared to a Rottweiler like Frankie.

He drained the last of his water and put his glass down on one of the thousand or so round white-linen-covered tables. Young boys were running around, playing chasing games and pretending to shoot one another. Kids were the same the world over.

It had been the same for him and his brother. Back in the day when the worst thing he could expect his brother to do was tell tales. Not steal his girlfriend. When the most competitive they'd been was over who could run from the stables to the indoor arena fastest.

Until it had become a game of who could net the prettiest girl. A game Mark had taken all too seriously. Danny shook his head. What a time that had been. He checked his hands again—still no fists. Still no bitter taste.

'Your wife asked me to tell you that she has retired for the evening.'

The message came from one of Salim's staff.

His wife. He felt an uncomfortable sensation in his gut. 'Is she all right?'

'Yes, sir—quite all right. But excessively tired. I believe she played with the youngest daughters and they would not let her rest.' He smiled slightly, nodded and bowed himself away.

Danny wanted to see her. Wanted to see her very, very badly.

She'd been playing with the kids. Of course she had. He loved that about her—she was so far removed from the overly painted two-dimensional women he so often had to spend time with at parties here. Which was probably why he spent most of his time working, or playing rugby, or even volunteering. The glitz could sometimes leave him cold.

He said his goodnights and made his way back through the palace. He had a good five-minute walk to get back to their apartments. What would Georgia have made of Ireland? he wondered. It was so far removed from here, or even London. And so many city girls would balk at the earthiness of the place—never mind the rain and the muck, the horses and the work.

He smiled. She'd probably roll up her sleeves and get on with it. That seemed to be her way.

Probably best not to continue with that line of thought, though—there was no chance it was going to happen. No. Georgia would be dropped off in London. She would not be going on with him to Ireland. What would be the point? For his mother to get her hopes up that he'd finally met a woman worth marrying? For his brother to judge and envy? For Frankie to bond with? Definitely not. It would just make the deconstruction of their marriage that much more difficult. Would serve absolutely no purpose whatsoever other than bring a little bit more of her company for him, because he did enjoy it. She'd lightened his days. So far.

He opened the door of the suite of rooms they'd been allocated. A salon, a study, bathrooms and a bedroom.

If Salim suspected them of cutting a business marriage he was being a sly old fox about it with this. It was fairyland—just as she'd like it. Oil lamps and candles lit a stardust path round the room.

He padded in and closed the door softly. There was no sound. Nothing. But he sensed her. He stood, just absorbing the night that fell around him here, the heady feminine presence, the soft, sultry air.

Sure she was in bed and sleeping, he slipped out of his shoes and went further in. The bedroom door was ajar. He moved noiselessly. She'd been awake for hours, playing her role to perfection, which couldn't have been easy. And though he was on top of his game, because of the negotiations, Georgia must have been using as much nervous energy as he had himself to hold her own with Salim and his family.

Salim's wife was no slacker on the intellectual front— a graduate of Cambridge Unversity, she had specialised in international law before giving it up to have children. Maybe one day Georgia would also give up her job looking after other people's children to look after her own.

The bathroom mirror displayed his frown quite clearly. There he went again, speculating on things that really had nothing to do with him. What *was* it with these crazy little daydreams? Probably just his usual overwhelming need to control everything and everyone around him. The more time he spent with her the more she was getting under his skin. It was that simple—while she was around she was just another variable for him to manage and control. As soon as she was back in her own world he'd lose the need to worry about her.

He braced his arms on yet more marble. What a day. He was bone-deep tired. He'd have a shower and then find a bit of floor to sleep on. They had another early start, checking over what the lawyers had scratched out, and then the rest of the day to relax. Assuming there was nothing to upset Salim.

He stepped into the shower, and with water coursing over his shoulders and soap stinging his eyes let his mind drift away again. He should be feeling—what? Elated? Ecstatic? He was washing himself at the end of a day he'd been working towards for years. He was so close he could see the ink dry, smell the money, live the dream.

He turned off the water and dragged a towel across his weary body. He'd neglected his fitness this past week—not that he was ever anything other than muscle and bone…the benefit of good genes and good health. But he couldn't fool himself that the way Georgia's eyes lit up when she had her hands on him and her mouth on him made him damn sure he'd go the extra mile to keep her happy.

He tossed the towel down into a basket. There he went again. Daydreaming. Probably sleep-deprived on top of everything else. He went back into the lounge. Only the lamps still flickered their light. He went to each and doused the wicks.

A space to sleep… He looked around. The sofas were not conducive to a man over six feet tall lying out. He looked at the floor—marble, overlaid with silk rugs here and there. He could suffer it—had slept on worse. He looked at the bedroom door, still ajar. Maybe there was another sofa in there, or at least some cushions he could put down.

He walked in. And stopped dead.

He was witnessing beauty—an oil-painted master-piece. Red hair tumbled across the pillow. Pale, fine fingers dangled off the edge of the bed. An arm was bared and a shoulder peeped above the fine coverlet. And her face was serene in sleep.

He stared. Traced the rest of her body's lines and curves under the shelter of the sheet. The dip of her waist, the long stretch of her leg, bent. Her breathing slow and peaceful.

He shook his head, smiled at his own weakness for her. A weakness he had clearly now mastered. He looked around for something—anything comfortable to lie on. Sat down on the edge of the huge bed, facing the door. Felt the weariness of his body. Twisted his sore muscles and laid himself down on the edge. Just five minutes and then he'd roll himself onto the floor.

He closed his eyes. *Heaven.*

CHAPTER EIGHT

SHOUTING, CHASING. HER CHEST bursting with each huge gulping breath. The pub in sight—please let me in, please let me in. Door—can't find. Staring through the clouded windows. Blank faces, no one seeing, no one hearing. Louder and louder, closer and closer. They were nearly upon her. Please help me, please...

Arms, wrapping, holding, soothing.

'Georgia... Georgia...'

She felt as if she was falling onto a huge warm bed. The urge to give in was so strong. She could let herself drown in this bed, in these arms. But where was she? Where was Babs? Where was home? She couldn't let herself sink like this. It was too easy, too tempting. Run away, keep running, until she could find home.

'Georgia, it's all right. You're all right. I've got you.'

She was nearly home. The voice—that voice—she knew it. But she couldn't quite trust, couldn't let go. No—not yet.

'It's okay. You're dreaming...it's all good.'

Startled, she opened her eyes. 'Danny?'

She felt the warm firm planes of his flesh against her cheek. He was holding her, wrapping her. Salving her.

'Shh...'

'Danny.'

She absorbed that strength. The scent. The cooling chill of satin skin. He grasped her head, smoothed and settled her. Her hands, she realised, were clutching at him. Just him—just skin. And soft body hair. She nuzzled into him, breathed and rubbed. Cat-like, she rubbed her face on him.

'You were dreaming. But you're all right now. I've got you.'

She knew that—he didn't need to tell her—but she loved hearing his voice, that low, lilting rumble. She felt better than she'd ever been. She felt...*safe*. Was that the word? Safe and content.

She nuzzled in closer. Of course she did. He was holding her almost fully enclosed. His legs were wrapped around hers. His arms were wrapped around her body, holding her close to him. He was easing her out of her terror. And she was loving being eased.

'Sweetheart...'

He was moving her, the tangle of a sheet the only thing tugging her legs out of his reach. The caress of his voice became darker. Her clutching hands began to smooth over him, absorbing every inch of his chest. Her fingers cruised over his nipples. Her lips followed. She trailed a path—hot and sweet and wet. *Hunger.* She hungered for him. Couldn't drag her greedy mouth away from him.

He cradled her head, tilted it up to face him. Stared for long full moments into her eyes. Two hands were holding her face up to his. Then he closed his eyes and his mouth powered down.

He thrust his tongue inside and heaved her body up to his. She felt the flood of desire assault her. She moaned his name and lifted herself closer to him. He was half lying, leaning back on one elbow, his torso naked, golden, ripped to perfection. She could almost clamber up each firm, delicious muscle. She rested her hands on his biceps, marvelling at the contrast of skin and shape and size. Moved up to his shoulders, then dipped forward to bite.

He grabbed her shoulders, pushed her back.

'Georgia, if you want to stop you have to do it now.' He looked like a tempest about to blow. Barely restrained control. Huge power—just held back. His eyes were wild like an electric storm in that hard, male face. Lips drawn back revealed a gleam of teeth.

'No, don't stop. I can't stop. I have to have you—I have to have *all* of you.' She'd never been surer of anything in her life.

He scooped his mouth over hers again, plundered, and she almost screamed with the fire he lit in her.

'Georgia!'

He pulled back again—gasped. A flush of heat, a sheen of sweat—even less control.

'If we do this… Remember what you said.'

She stared into those eyes that were focussed so surely on hers. He was concerned—he really was. She'd been so clear, so sure. Knowing each other in this way would be stepping out into the dark, over the abyss. But she couldn't help wanting and needing him. She'd fought it for so long. She knew the consequences. She was going to suffer the consequences. But for now she was going to reap the rewards.

'I know what I want—I know what I'm doing. I can't stop this. I don't want to stop. Oh, Danny—please make love to me. *Please!*'

His body became like all the elements to her—essential as air, fire and water. He moved over her with a sense of powerful peace and she knew that, like her, he was relishing every second they had. His hands and mouth slowly took possession of every inch. His kiss slowed like lapping waves on the hottest day. His fingers trailed heat and light across her, melting and inciting her.

On and on, over and over, the glow of passion stoked and burned and stoked and burned. She needed him, breathed him, licked at him and dragged hands and nails and teeth over him.

The core between her legs was throbbing, pulsing— she'd become like an animal, lost all her layers of civilisation. She *was* her body and she gave it to him.

And he took.

He rose up, cradled her head and burned her with his eyes. She sank into his powerful hold. 'Georgia, you are the most beautiful woman I have ever met. Inside and out.'

He said the words like a prayer or a mantra, and then he began to worship her all over again. His mouth to her mouth, urgent now. His hands to the tiny nightdress she wore, lifting the satin up and over her head. Touching her down each arm, over her belly and up again to cup her aching breasts. Mouth dipping to suckle her, to bite her nipple gently, massaging her need higher and higher.

She reached for him but he held her back, one hand gripping her wrists, then pushed her down onto the bed. He stood over her as if she were his sacrifice. This was different from before—no games. Imbued with her spirit and her soul. She was truly offering herself, aching for the sense she knew she'd feel of something higher, deeper, more fulfilling.

He stood tall, erect. All man. His thighs were thick and long and her gaze rested on the huge bulge between them. She reached up but he pushed her down again. Shook his head and smiled at her.

'Patience, Georgia.'

But as he pulled off his tight boxers her tongue snaked out involuntarily over her lips. He was so ready for her, his body thrumming with excitement.

'You want to put the condom on?'

She shook her head and watched as he rolled it on in one swift movement. She touched herself—couldn't not as he stood ready before her, the most potent, masculine image she had ever seen. From the fierce gaze to the lines of his shoulders to his powerful stance.

He watched her fingers stroke herself and then he covered her hand and touched her too. She was so aroused. 'You blow my mind, beautiful girl.'

He leaned forwards and would have given her what she needed there, but she wanted him properly—now. With a fierce impatience she'd never known before.

She grabbed his head and urged him up. Leaned back on her elbows. He braced his arms by her sides. She fell back on the bed and he kissed her. She reached her arms up round his neck, ran her fingers through the soft short waves of his hair. Their mouths melded, her legs fell open and he rested his weight on the bed.

Her hands ran along the cords of muscle in his shoulders. She felt his hands, his body, his length brush against her as he settled himself. The anticipation redoubled with each touch, sending darts of hot joy. And then he entered her. He was big and swift, but she was so ready. Her eyes flew to his and he stilled long enough to check her.

'Am I hurting you?'

He was so big, so long and yes it had hurt for a moment, but nothing would stop this now.

'You're perfect. Perfect, Danny.'

Her hips rose up and she urged him on. He pushed inside again and pulled back, stroked her aching core with each thrust. Again and again, building and quickening.

She loved. She gave. And then she angled her hips a little more and felt the nerves inside her begin to quiver in an inferno of heat.

He was calling her name, building them up, pushing and throbbing. She felt her nipples rub on his chest. She felt the huge sexual power he incited in her body. And then her mind cleared and her heart surged and she was flying on the crest of the biggest wave as her orgasm built and built and finally burst. She screamed as she clung to him and he stoked her on and on.

Never. She had never known pleasure like this. Her whole body was convulsing in waves around him.

And then he stilled. Still rolling from waves of pleasure, she watched the strain across his face, then the pleasure as he surrendered to his own shuddering climax. She clung to his back as his release bucked him. The sheen of their sweat, the sensation of their coupling weighing on her like a precious mantle she never wanted to take off.

Wrapping them together, he rolled her over and they lay entwined on the bed, breath steadying, hearts easing.

'I knew it would be amazing, Georgia. I knew it from the moment I saw you walk into that hotel.'

She felt his heart thud and then step into a strong, steady rhythm under her cheek.

'You drew every eye—always do—everywhere you go. Not just your looks, your sensuality. Not just those surface things. You've got something, Georgia—something very special.'

He reached for her hand, clasped it and held it between them. She laced her fingers in his and found she didn't want to speak, just to listen.

He held her for a long time, languorous, giving her the easy come-down that she needed. How long would it take her to recover? she wondered. How would she ever recover?

Finally—how long later? Five minutes? Ten? Forty? She had no idea, but she needed to feel him again. She kissed his chest, wriggled out of his grasp and lay spooned with him while he held her close. Their bodies were slick and musky and she felt that animalistic vital throb begin again. Lying like this? She had never lain like this before. Never.

'Sweetheart, you okay?'

She shook her head. Finally she found her voice, the power of speech. 'After that—nothing. It was the best. I'm just loving lying here, Danny. Nothing to do except... enjoy it. No pressure, no need to go anywhere, do anything. I don't even think I could if I had to.'

'We have to do a few things, but we can spend a whole lot of time just doing this if that suits you. Suits me. I can think of nothing better. *Nothing.*'

'Mmm...'

She curled and luxuriated like a cat on a hearth. It was beyond gorgeous to be held like this. With the feeling of security and sanctuary. And home. Why did that word keep flying into her mind? Was it the dream? Was it her guilt about Babs? She longed to go home, of course she did...

'What sort of things do we have to do?'

He snaked a hand under her arm, found her breast. 'We have to do this all over again. A few times.'

He circled his finger round, not touching her nipple, and she arched into him, needing the burn.

'Good—*good.* We can do that. Oh, yes, let's do that.'

'I'm not sure if you're ready yet.'

He cupped her breast now, idly flicked his thumb across the tip of her nipple.

'*Are* you ready? So soon?'

She stilled and absorbed each gentle lash. Lapped it up. Felt him pulse and harden between her legs. A cry escaped her throat. He was fast—panther-fast. Moved her just where he wanted her. Whipped her round, face down on the bed. Legs spread and ass tilted up for him.

He was sheathed and slipping inside her, and then he rode her. One hand on her hip, one hand on her breast, he pounded into her. Hard, demanding thrusts. She twisted her head to see him, so proud and male and in control. Until he began to come, and then she knew her power. His eyes found hers and his face broke. She pushed back, to get even more from each thrust, and rubbed herself against him to her own blinding climax.

They collapsed down in the same spoon position as before, gasping and laughing. 'Wow, Georgia. That was *fast*. I didn't know a woman could go so fast.'

'I didn't know I could go so fast either. It's a new speed for me.'

He smoothed her back. 'Suits you.'

'Yeah, I'm happy with it. Though we *could* go for medium next?'

'I reckon we could.'

They lay still.

'What time do you think it is?'

'Time Salim wanted us to spend together. He's on to us, I'm sure. But we're playing along beautifully.'

She stretched up onto her arms and looked down at this man, so strong and yet sometimes so brittle. He lay there right now, basking in his own strength, his arms crossed behind his head, and she knew he'd got the whole world lined up just as he wanted it. His deal and her.

She'd succumbed and she was glad. The fallout would happen—of course it would—but these moments she would treasure. For him it might just be more frosting on the sweetest deal—a taste and then move on to another morsel. She knew how many beautiful girls there were out here, all living as if time was running through their fingers, as if tomorrow the party might be over so today they'd give it their all. He'd replace her in a heartbeat. But now that she'd bitten the apple she'd take her fill.

She leaned down to kiss the mouth that had worshipped her. Full-lipped, fully expert.

'So he's on to us?'

'Yeah. I think so. I've never met a sharper man. Or one more humble. Despite his wealth.' He spread out his arms. 'I mean just look at this—it's beyond wealth. It's majestic. But do you see anyone here acting anything other than respectfully?'

She shrugged, still propped up beside him. He circled her pale slim arm with his hand, ran it up and down.

'That takes some effort—to get his whole family to act responsibly and respectfully. It's all too easy to lose track of basics when the money flows so readily.'

'Money flowing easily has never been a problem where I came from.' She laughed.

He reached up to cup her cheek. 'You have so much to treasure, Georgia. And I know you do treasure it. I never hear you bleat or moan about not having your parents.'

She turned her face into his palm, kissed it.

'I could never complain about what I had. I'm so grateful. I could have had no one. Babs could have acted like any other teenager might have done in that situation.'

She let her fingers trail along the line of his ribcage, down one side, back up, down the other. So smooth, with hair circling and descending from his navel.

'It's more the wondering *what if?* Hoping that if I ever have a family of my own they'll have as good an upbring-

ing—and more. Everything I can give them. And some
of the things I never had—like two parents.'

She swallowed. Almost shocked by what she had just
admitted. Her own private little dream. But she knew he
wouldn't belittle her. She risked a glance. But what she
saw wasn't a benign look of empathy. It was clouded,
hard to read, troubled. And it lasted a long moment between them.

'Yeah, well, your upbringing and mine...different, but
we're each grateful for what we had. Until, in my case,
I messed it up.'

She swallowed the instant question. If he was going
to talk this was the closest he'd ever come...

'I owe you an explanation. About some of the stuff
you've seen this past couple of days.'

She stayed still. Very still. Didn't want to distract him.
It was like those precious moments when a vulnerable
child finally trusted her enough to say that his mum never
fed him, or his dad was violent, or described whatever
personal hell he was going through. When that arc of
trust connected you could do nothing to jeopardise it.

'We—my brother and I—were quite close once. Never
as close as me and Frankie, but just normal—like you'd
expect any two brothers growing up in rural Ireland to
be. Though when I say rural Ireland don't misunder-
stand me—we had a privileged upbringing. Everything
we could want. And by that I mean freedom, as well as
all the love and material stuff.'

'It does sound idyllic.' What else could she say?

'It was. Though there was always an edge—a competitive edge—between me and Mark. I'd like to say it
was balanced, but...' He cut his glance away, to the sofa,
to the window, to the terrace outside and the morning
that was already blazing desert-hot. 'But for me it be-

came all. I *had* to win—every time. And nearly every time I did. Mark was older, and he saw my "issues", if you want to call it that, so maybe he let me win…maybe not. But the one time when it really counted—when I had something I wanted more than anything else—that was when he stopped indulging me and went for it himself. Maya. My girlfriend.'

'He tried to take her for himself?'

Danny kept his head turned but she could see the clouds chasing over his face. Finally he spoke. 'He succeeded.'

'And that was the biggest game to win?'

'It wasn't a game. It was real. She was with *me*. Had been for years—since we were fourteen—and then it just seemed to happen. They both sat me down one day and told me that they'd got together. It was like your parents telling you they're going to divorce, I imagine. I couldn't believe it—*wouldn't* believe it—and then when I had to believe it I acted in the only way I knew how. I went for him. Blind drunk. *Really* went for him. It took three of my friends to pull me off him. And he wouldn't fight back, which made it worse, so…'

He looked round at her, up at her, but it was as if he didn't really see her. He was reliving this horror from the past.

'So I did quite a bit of damage—blue lights, mother distraught. I'd caught Mark at an angle and ruptured his spleen. Huge internal bleeding. I stayed long enough to know he was going to pull through and then I left on a flight to London that night. Stayed there—laboured, got a degree in engineering—then four years later came here to Dubai. And that was it.'

He looked at her—properly this time. 'So now you

know. I nearly killed my own brother in a jealous rage. *Not* something you really want to put on your CV.'

She lay down beside him, hoping he'd get some comfort from the heat of her body, still not quite sure of the words that would make him stop this self-hatred.

He didn't touch her. She didn't attempt to touch him. The bridge of trust could still be so easily crumbled. She'd let him take the lead.

'Funny… Up until yesterday—' he turned his face, so close she could see the navy flecks in his eyes '—and I mean yesterday—I couldn't even say their names without having a physical reaction. My own shame, but still the anger, like a beast. You've no idea, Georgia, how much work it took for me not to punch the nearest wall whenever I heard their names.'

She ventured a slight move towards him. She needed to as much for her own sake as his now. 'I think I saw that in Indigo. When Ciaran teased you about marrying before your brother.'

She trailed a finger lightly down his arm. He didn't flinch or move away.

'Knowing all this now—I suppose you handled it as well as you could.'

He swallowed. 'Maybe. But it still wasn't great. People should be able to ask me about my family without me erupting and walking out.'

She took another risk—put her arms across his chest and laid her head there too. He shifted, but it was to wrap her up, to cradle her.

'And you brought it all out again. The jealousy. It's still there, even after all this time and all those months of…' he put his fingers up, made air quotes '…"working things through". Imagining scenarios and working out solutions before they happened. Didn't work *you* out, though, did they?'

She scooted right over him. Their nakedness was now as easy as breathing. She straddled him, held the sides of his face, and looked long and deep into those eyes.

'You're so honest—with yourself, with me. And you've got more skill and talent and energy than anyone I've ever met.' She dipped down to kiss him. 'You've already conquered nearly every demon. You've pulled us out of a near disaster, you've netted this deal...' She sat up, looked round at the room they were in. 'You're a part of this world now, Danny. One day you'll have a home like this too—one day soon!'

'A palace can be a mausoleum, Georgia—if the right people aren't in it.'

Those words she let slide right over her. He didn't mean *her*. So she wouldn't get all caught up in what he did mean. She would do instead what came very naturally, very easily, and kiss him.

The photo call was arranged for after lunch. A crew had arrived—big enough, it seemed, to make a movie never mind take a picture.

Hair and make-up already done, Georgia walked into the state room which had been allocated for the shoot. Sheikh Salim, his wife, who had been utterly, perfectly charming, and their children were all going to be pictured.

The whole event was being seen as the first publicity for this project—United Arab Leisure—and the construction of facilities that would be world-leading for every conceivable sport, every necessary environment. And as well as the usual leisure facilities and shopping malls that were part and parcel of UAE life there would be jobs created for five thousand workers—well-paid jobs, with good conditions, accommodation and education. No more slave labour.

These two giants of Dubai society were combining forces to ensure it. Salim's wealth and Danny's ingenuity.

And the PR icing? A wedding. With the perfect bride.

Georgia wore white. Not blinding virginal white but a soft ivory dress and jacket. Fitted, elegant, off the peg, but still so much more than she could have ever afforded before. She had dressed with a tinge of sadness. This would possibly be her one and only wearing of this outfit. She didn't think she'd have the heart to give it another airing. And Babs was a totally different body shape, so it wasn't as if *she* could take this and the other clothes. A charity shop donation would possibly be best...

They arranged themselves in the state room. Salim sat on a throne-like chair in full traditional dress, his wife to his left. To his right, catching her eye as soon as he walked through the door, was Danny. He wore the darkest grey, the whitest shirt and a tie with flashes of blue almost as vibrant as his eyes. His hair was tidy and his face clean-shaven. And he wore a look that told the world he was in charge.

She took her place beside him, in a constant state of minor turmoil that she was living a lie—albeit a temporary one. This event should be about their deal, the good news, the progress, but it was being overshadowed by a wedding that was already on its descent path.

'You look beautiful, Mrs Ryan. I can hardly make out the dark circles under your eyes...' he murmured into her ear.

'Thank you, Mr Ryan. Your own scrubbing up has produced excellent results also.'

They had stayed in bed until forced to get up at midday. From waking in the early hours they had made love. Then dozed off and on. She didn't think it would have been possible to tune her body to his any more, or for her to have had greater pleasure than she'd had—than he'd given her. And she knew that if they'd had the whole day free they would have still been in bed. She'd known the sexual chemistry between them was good—amazing— but it had been above and beyond her wildest dreams. And there. Time to burst another happiness bubble.

A journalist had booked some time with them. Time to rehash their tried and tested story. What Georgia *hadn't* counted on was a reference to the photographs taken at the Al-Jafar.

'So the world first learned about your romance when pictures of you were released causing an internet sensation?'

Georgia stared blankly. This wasn't supposed to be an investigative piece—it was an exclusive feature for a glossy magazine—so she should have had no fear that she would be under any real scrutiny.

She opened her mouth to rebuff the question, but Danny cut in first.

'Indeed. We would have preferred that this photo shoot was our first—however, not every journalist is as scrupulous as those working at your magazine. So rumours arose and our preferred option was not to comment— lending weight to idle gossip is not my preferred MO. What else would you like to talk about?'

Photo shoot, interview and all pretence over, Danny strode through the palace, loosening his tie and growling.

'I should have briefed them in advance. They should have been told what was and what wasn't off-limits.'

He paused, realising that she couldn't keep up with him in her heels and tight dress.

'Sorry, Georgia. I can't believe I didn't see that one coming. You weren't too thrown?'

'I'm fine,' she replied, catching up as he waited at the door to their suite. 'You can't see everything coming, Danny. Some things just happen, despite all the risk assessments you do. Life can't always go according to your schedules and plans.'

He strode ahead again, wrenching off the tie, tossing it down on the back of a sofa, sloughing off his jacket and discarding it with barely more care onto a chair.

'Not in *my* world. Life goes entirely to plan. That way there's no room for error. And when a curveball *does* come you make another plan.'

She slipped out of her shoes, took off her rings and placed them on the coffee table. Almost casually.

'Like this? This whole fake marriage?'

She didn't wait for an answer. She was tired. Tired of keeping up appearances, tired after making love for hours and tired of the emotions that were rolling through her. Worry, anxiety, shame, guilt…and the growing feelings she had for Danny. Feelings that she now knew for certain were going to be with her long after this wedding weekend had passed.

He stood watching her, clearly taken aback by her comment. 'Yes, exactly like this.'

'Sorry,' she said. 'I'm just being churlish. And grumpy.'

She walked through to the shower, turned it on. Took off her pretty silk satin jacket and dress, hung them carefully on their hanger and stood in her underwear, looking at him.

He was following her about, frowning. 'It's a bit late now to say you're unhappy.'

She sighed. 'I'm not saying that. I'm just trying to make a point that not everything will always go to plan—and this is a clear example. I mean, I knew that we shouldn't sleep together, but we did—and there wasn't a plan in the world that would have stopped that happening.'

'Are you regretting that too?'

She aimed for nonchalance, tied up her hair, took off her earrings. Tried hard not to be cowed by the blast from his furnace.

'No, Danny. I'm not. How could I regret one second of it? It was amazing. And I'll deal with the fallout—in time.'

He walked over to her in two strides, catching up with her as she was about to go into the shower. 'You're not the only one who's going to experience the fallout, Georgia. I'm in this with you, and what we've done—joining forces for the business as well as the physical side—it's been…amazing.'

The bathroom was steamy. Her head was muggy.

He followed her right in.

'I know that it's not going to just disappear the minute we go our separate ways. I can't even look at you in your underwear or let you go for a shower without wanting to grab you and make love to you. So I'm fully with you on that.'

He turned on the full force of his presence. She was getting the whole works. She knew his ways well enough now to know that he saved this for when he *really* wanted something. Question was—what did he want?

'Georgia…'

He moved towards her, still in shirt and trousers, but looking dishevelled and sexy and hot. Was he thinking she'd need some super-persuasion to want to sleep with him again? Because even if her common sense told her not to her body had been lit up from within and already craved and responded to his presence—never mind his touch.

'I think we have more talking to do. I think we should have a proper discussion—about us.' He started to un-button his shirt. 'Later.'

She should be stronger. She should tell him that they didn't need to discuss anything. What would be the point? If she was cynical she would say it might at best be an attempt for him to keep his little Georgia ducks lined up. But she was weak where Danny Ryan was concerned.

Her sense of self-preservation had to be strong, though. And she'd already decided that she would have this indulgence, pay the price, draw a line and then move on. Just how long all that would take was the unknown quantity.

'Georgia… That lovely silk underwear is going to get all wet.'

He was completely out of his clothes now. *Virile*. That was what she saw when she looked at him.

'It's already wet.'

She didn't mean it to sound in any way enticing. But the gleam in his eyes told her he'd taken it that way. He took another step towards her, took off her bra and pant-ies and took her in the shower.

CHAPTER NINE

SOMETHING WAS UP. A missed call from Mark. It had been years since they had even been in the same room, and he was calling now—leaving a voicemail? Danny stared at the phone in his hand as if he'd never seen it before, surprised that he didn't want to hurl it into a wall.

He hadn't even recognised the number, but the minute the message began to play and he'd heard that voice…

'Danny, hi. It's me, Mark—I wonder if you would give me a call back, I'm worried…'

He'd clicked it off. Hadn't been able to bring himself to listen to any more.

He looked out of the window to the lap pool on his terrace. *His* terrace. *His* house. Showpiece of everything he'd worked so hard to achieve. Designed for him and every dirham paid by him through the blood, sweat and tears of ten years in the desert. Ten years proving that he amounted to more than the human volcano who'd nearly killed his own brother.

He'd built up an empire out here—he was respected, admired, valued. And he'd just put the cherry on top of the whole damn cake. The Sheikh's deal was signed, sealed and soon to be delivered. They'd got the whole thing wrapped up within two days and then he'd brought Georgia back here. Back here to get things organised, get her stuff packed, say goodbye to her girlfriends and her kindergarten kids and get all her other loose ends tied up in a neat little bow.

Four days. Four intoxicating days.

He'd thought having her in his house would become cloying, annoying—and in time, of course, it would. She was the first woman even to make it past his front door. But the sweet, hot thrill of her sweet, hot body next to his whenever he wanted it was still doing it for him. He had even been prepared to take off for a few days. Whatever she fancied—Indian Ocean, Europe, even one of the spa hotels out in the desert. But, no, she'd been resolute. Even determined. Her heart belonged to London. She was pining for her sister and the rain!

He knew she was right. The sand timer was trickling with borrowed time—there were only days left before the last grains fell and their lives as they'd known them before started up again.

Georgia.

She walked out onto the terrace, right up to the pool and dived in. Sleek and skilled. As she was at everything. He watched her strike out in steady lengths, up and down. Then she leaned on the edge, pushed herself up and out and just as gracefully emerged, dripping onto the deck. She twisted her hair into a coil and wrung it out. Brushed drips off her legs with her hands and then turned, caught him staring, and flashed him that big toothy grin.

What was he supposed to do with *that*? It was a smile that instantly made him smile right back. A flash of that body that instantly made him want to grab it. He lifted his arm and waved.

She gestured for him to come out and join her. In their two days at Salim's and the four days here he'd joined her in almost everything. It had been as close to a honeymoon as he could let his mind wrap itself around.

He'd got all caught up in the party atmosphere at the palace. Slipping more and more away from who he really was into who he was pretending to be. A happily married man. A man who believed in the sanctity of marriage. A man who had promised himself and the world that he'd put his faith and trust in one woman.

But he couldn't live that mirage. He could never trust again. The only person he could rely on was himself. And the jealous rages he'd felt flaring up when he'd been with her told him he might not be able to truly rely on himself either. The only option was the life he'd once had—Al-Jafar penthouse weekends with no-strings-attached women. And it had served him pretty well up until one week ago.

She was still staring at him, smiling blithely, expectantly. She grabbed up the bottle of sun cream that was never far away and held it out, turned her back to him, mouthed the words *Rub cream on my back* and winked coyly over her shoulder.

That was the problem. He'd like nothing more. That silky skin, his cream-slicked hands slipping all over it, right down to her bikini briefs, under, smoothing over her perfect cheeks and then up, laying her down, undoing her bikini, massaging her breasts, tightening her nipples... And then nothing surer than slipping his hand between her legs and rubbing her hot, wet bud into a hot, wet climax.

His hand gripped the phone. Tightly. He wanted her so badly it frightened him.

But that voicemail had pierced the dream—burned like acid. Reminded him of home and heartache. And, much as he hated it, he had to deal with it. Whatever Mark had called to say, it had to be important.

He shook his head, held the phone up, mouthed *On a call*, turned away. The slight slip of her smile was a harsh jab to his gut. And there would be more to come.

He pressed the missed call's number and waited. Something close to nausea bubbled inside him.

A dial tone.

That voice.

'Mark Ryan.'

'You called me. What for?'

A pause.

'Hey, Danny. Thanks for phoning back. It's good to hear from you.'

'Yeah? Get to the point.'

Another pause. The bile in his throat was just staying down—*just*.

A sigh. 'It's Frankie. Nothing to panic about. I'm sure she's all right. But…'

'But what?' He felt himself slip into anger, felt the beast in his stomach growl. 'What's wrong?' he demanded.

'Look, would you just calm down? Nothing is wrong—nothing that I can be sure of. Yet. I think she's gone to ground. And I think you're probably the only one she'll turn to.'

He swallowed. And again. Breathed in through his nose. Out. Calm.

'Tell me more.'

'There's not much to tell. She was on a business trip and hooked up with that guy Hermida. Went off-radar for almost a month. Next thing we see her tagged in a photo in Argentina, looking like death. Maya messaged her and got a two-word response: I'm fine. That's it. But we know she's *not* fine. That was a week ago. And no-one's heard anything since.'

Which made it the same day that he'd got married. The same day that Frankie had messaged him to give him her usual blast of derision. Then the softer text message later. That was concerning in itself.

'I've kept Mum out of it—you know how she panics.'

That much was true. He'd never forget the look on her face when she'd seen her number one son getting a life-saving blood transfusion. That image would live with him always. He'd done that. Was solely responsible. Anyone else would have talked it through—or not…maybe decided on no communication at all. But a full-blown physical attack? He still felt the shame and disgust.

'By the way—I hear congratulations are in order.'

'Congratulations? You heard wrong.' The crack of his voice was like a whiplash. 'I'll be in touch.'

He clicked off the phone. Tossed it down onto the sofa. Turned at a sound at the door. Georgia. Questions and hurt in her eyes…ghostly pale.

'Are you—? Is everything all right?'

'It's fine.'

She stood at the door—he stood at the window. He stared at her, at the phone he'd thrown down, feeling the giant come-down begin for real.

'You don't seem fine.'

He could feel himself wavering. Georgia could be his rock, his support. He could tell her what was up and she would listen and share and offer insight. She would come and wind her lissom body into his, holding on to him and imbuing him with her warmth and care…

And she would lead him to a place he'd sworn he'd never go again—trusting a woman. Nothing good would come of it. So he'd better snap himself out of that nice, cosy little scene.

'Danny?'

The care in her voice was syrup-thick.

'Look, it's nothing I want to talk about. I have calls to make, but they don't concern you.'

He looked up sharply, his eyes following his voice, already wincing and recoiling at his own callousness. He'd expected to see her walk away, unprepared to put up with those harsh words. But she was standing there, Joan of Arc in a green bikini, unflinching, unmoving. Steady.

'I know you well enough now to know that something pretty major is bothering you. Is it the Sheikh? Has something gone wrong with the contract?'

'It's got nothing to do with the contract. It's…it's something else.'

He could cave. He could so easily let her into his life. She was shimmering with strength and kindness and part of him longed to share this with her. She'd never let him down yet, and even when he had been an idiot before she'd handled herself—and him—so well. She'd helped him navigate through one of the biggest moments of his life. She was amazing…perfect. But he had so much to lose. So little to win.

Risky. It was too risky. She was drawing him like a siren onto rocks that he knew were treacherous. He had to cut her loose, keep her back, keep his distance. Give himself time to figure this out. He needed to focus on Frankie for now. Later he'd sit down and give this whole thing some thought. Maybe it *could* work? Maybe… But now wasn't the time to start making decisions.

'Georgia, I appreciate that you're trying to be helpful but I don't want your help. And I don't need it. Thanks.'

She nodded. Slightly. Still holding it together.

'I understand.'

No sulk, no drama. Just dignity. She smiled…softly and sadly. As if she was throwing a white rose on the coffin of an old friend. And then she turned and walked away. The quiet flip-flop of her feet faded. The space contracted to fit only him again.

He stood for a second. It was all he could spare.

Frankie was in trouble.

He grabbed up his phone again. He would start with the simplest thing first. He dialled her number.

It went straight to voicemail.

He moved to his laptop. Fired it up, entered his password, opened up all the social media tabs, every email account, searched for her. He found the photo that Mark had told him about. His beautiful sister's short dark hair was in its usual curtains round her face, but the hollows and shadows and the gloom in her eyes told him she was in pain.

*If anyone has hurt her…*he thought, trying to call Rocco Hermida to mind. The arrogant Argentinian had come to the stables years ago, toured around the stud ponies like some exotic Prince of Darkness. He'd only been a couple of years older than him but had acted as if he was in a whole different league. Had Frankie fallen for it—for *him*? He racked his brains. Maybe. It was round about that time when he'd noticed that she was actually a girl.

He messaged her in every format he knew. He searched for Hermida online, to see what he could find out. Apart from a constant stream of models, actresses and It Girls, he was into mergers and acquisitions. And polo. At all levels—breeding, playing and financing.

He called the contacts he had in the polo world. He made notes, and lists, came at it from every angle. He began to close in on where she was…what they'd done. He was almost ready to phone Mark back.

He looked down at his hands—steady. He swallowed—no acid. He called up a mental image—Maya… with Mark. Nothing. *Nothing.* He felt self-satisfaction. He nodded.

And then he heard a noise. Georgia.

'Hey.'

It was dark. She was dressed. She was carrying two glasses of wine. She looked like a goddess in jeans.

'You've been sitting here for ages. I thought you might want a little sustenance.'

She put one glass down and moved back. He noticed that lamps were lit all through the house. He looked through the plate-glass walls that pretty much made up half of the hard fabric of the building, could see past the TV lounge and the dining area through to the kitchen. He could smell food.

'Have you been cooking? You're an angel.'

He reached for her glass. Took it out of her hands, placed it next to his and pulled her down onto his lap. Kissed her long and slow. Told her with his mouth how much he admired her, how much he wanted her, how much he adored her. She snaked herself round him and rubbed herself against him in that cat-like way she had, almost purring.

They were going to make love again.

It had been hours since they'd done it last. Hours while he'd sorted out his head, sorted out this mess and begun to see that there was a good chance of this enforced contact with Mark having some kind of positive outcome.

He pulled her hair out of its ponytail, eased it down and smoothed it through his hands, loving the soft weight, the sweet scent. Maybe it was her presence that had made such a difference to the way he was coping with this. He was able to think about his brother without the intense physical reaction that had plagued him for years. Even after all that therapy it was only in the past week that he'd actually been able to hold the images in his mind without feeling his control slip.

He kissed her. He was able to focus on the here, the now, on the beautiful woman in his arms, without letting his mind be tainted with the shame of what he'd done— or nearly done. He was actually as close as he could ever imagine to mastering this.

But what if he felt that rage again for someone else— for Georgia?

He really, *really* needed to start puzzling out what he was going to do about her. Having her in his lap…in his life—it was too precious just to give it up without a proper analysis.

He kissed her smooth brow, her chin, her nose, her lips. He fed his hand up under her top. Watched her arch her back and stretch her neck in response. Every move she made fuelled him further. He wanted to roll her onto her back, but this room was all hard edges. He lost himself in her kisses. She was so easy to share moments with, so accepting. But still he owed her an apology.

'Georgia… Earlier…'

She sat back on his lap, held his head between her hands. Smiled and shook her head.

'It doesn't matter.'

'It does. I need to explain. The call—it was from home. From Mark. It freaked me out a bit. But it's sorted now. I think. This whole thing with my brother has taken up so much of my life. I've told you bits of it, but I should—'

She put her finger over his lips, hushed him. Followed

it with her lips. Kissed him deeply. As deeply as he could remember. Soul-deep. He felt the air shift. Found succour.

She pulled back, pressing little kisses. She rubbed her nose gently on his. One more long, deep kiss. Then back she sat.

'It doesn't matter. Really it doesn't. Because I'm going home. I'm not going to bother you, try to coax you…'

He jerked back, grabbed her wrists.

'What do you mean, you're going home?'

She glanced back over her shoulder and he saw that as well as the beautiful, architecturally designed villa, with its glass, mahogany and private views of the Gulf, there were three pieces of matching luggage and a hand-bag—all stacked up beside one another.

She swung her head back and looked at his face. Her eyes were as dark and fathomless as serpentine jade.

'Danny. It's time for me to go. I can't seem to help you. You think I'm just a mother hen, clucking round you. You hate me fussing—hate exploring your emotions. You're… We're just… I don't know—made differently.'

He watched her lips move but he wasn't really hearing her.

'So what's going on here? You've opened a bottle of wine and packed your bags? You think we're going to kiss goodbye and then you'll jump a cab? What have I to do? Watch TV and eat pasta? Is that it?'

She stood up, stepped back. Her face cast a shadow he'd never seen before.

'And that's the other reason I'm going. Your temper. I don't deserve it. No one does. But me least of all—because all I've done is play my part in this, and played it well.'

He stood up. Faced her. The white lights of a car—a cab?—beamed through the night, rivalling the glow of the lamps and the blaring computer and TV screens. Cut in through his home and severed what was left of his peace.

'Don't be crazy. You can't just walk out now, swinging your handbag and rolling your damn suitcases. We've got stuff to talk about.'

His head hurt. Days and nights with so little sleep. The stress and tension of his business, his brother. His sister doing a vanishing act. And now this.

'Talking won't change the facts now. It's well past time I was gone.'

'No. Not yet. You're not going in that cab. Call the driver. Tell him you made a mistake.'

'No.'

He felt his jaw ache.

'Danny, this was never for ever. This *was* what it was. We both knew that. And I see more and more every day that we're not good for each other. You can't handle someone like me.'

His jaw felt wired. *He* knew what he needed.

'What the hell do you mean, someone like you?'

She put her hands on her hips. 'Someone who's not going to fall into line and do what they're told! Someone who wants to talk through problems and find solutions—someone who won't put up with you snarling at people when things don't go to plan. And as for the plans! You think every single thing fits into a box. And if it doesn't you blast it—until it bends into shape or melts out of sight.'

He could feel his eyebrows somewhere up near his hairline. He could feel his mouth hanging open. No one spoke to him like this. *No one.* With the exception of his sister, maybe. But she was deep in some Argentinian township with her own problems. And he still hadn't phoned Mark back. He had to get on with that—had to get this nonsense knocked on the head.

Georgia was going nowhere—not at this time of night and not on these terms. She was out of her mind if she thought that.

'Georgia. We entered into a partnership—a contract. As far as I'm concerned it's not over until we both say so. And…' he checked his watch '…eleven p.m. on a Friday is not close of contract time. Not by *my* watch.'

'My cab is waiting and your sauce is burning.'

Now he shook his head. 'My *sauce* is burning?'

'Yes. You're doing your blasting thing at me, trying to get me in line, and now your sauce is burning!'

His 'blasting thing'?

She looked more magnificent than mutinous. He stepped aside to let her pass. She marched—marched and stomped—through to the kitchen. He went out into the night. The air was as hot as he could remember. He shoved a bundle of notes to the cab driver and sent him off. Turned to go back up to the house.

She was standing there. And if he'd thought he'd seen all her regal looks he'd never seen this one. Every inch of her posture was pulled tight and perfect. Head high, neck long, shoulders back. Poised as if she was about to command a fleet. Her suitcases were the only thing out of alignment—she'd actually started rolling them to the door.

'Get me another cab. I've got an hour to get to the airport.'

'I've told you—not tonight.'

'And I told you I'm going. I'm not going to listen to you any more.'

'Georgia, whether or not we'd had a fight earlier, I still wouldn't be letting you head off to the airport at this time of night on your own. It's just not happening. Deal with it.'

'A fight? You couldn't call that a *fight*, Danny—it was just another one-sided blast from you to whoever was in your path.'

She didn't even seem angry about it—she just seemed acknowledging.

'It happened to be me. And the longer I hang around, the more blasts I'll be expected to suffer.' She sighed. 'So I *am* going to go. I've booked a flight. It's for the best.'

All he could do was look at her.

'We both knew this moment was going to come at the end of this week. Whether we were in London or here or wherever. It's what we agreed.'

He couldn't accept it. He knew he must, but he could not accept it. Wasn't quite ready to.

'In the morning… I'll take you myself in the morning.'

She sighed again. 'Morning means another night together. It means more of what bonds us. And that's not going to help.' She shook her head. 'We should never have been intimate so quickly. It's clouded everything.'

Georgia Anne Blue. The hottest woman he had ever met. He couldn't imagine being anything other than intimate with her—it clouded nothing.

'Anyway, I've paid for a ticket.'

'Georgia, you're a freaking millionaire. You can afford another.'

She looked at him then, and then down at her feet. He should have seen this one coming.

'You're not going to keep the money, are you? You're going to make some noble gesture and give it back—or give it to charity. That would be so *you*, Georgia.'

He shook his head. He should have known. While he'd spent his life working for the next big break, the next

badge to show how far he'd come, it was all surface—
all show. She wanted to go back to a pub in London and
the warmth and love of her tiny family. *His* family? He
couldn't get further away from them if he tried. Even
his sister. Even the one person who'd made an effort to
keep the bridges intact between them for all these years.
She was on another continent, in trouble, and he was the
last to know.

'I'll clear my sister's debts and give you the rest back. I
don't want… I can't tell Babs what I've done. What *we've*
done. I'll make something up about the sixty thousand.
It's great that I can help her out with that at least. I've
thought about it. I can say I got a big bonus—that the
kindergarten parents can be crazy generous at times. I
don't know…something like that.'

'And us? What are you going to tell her about us?'

He saw a wobble then. She couldn't look at him.

She grabbed the strap of her handbag tighter, reached
down for the handle of another piece of her luggage. 'She
won't ask much if she thinks I'm upset. But I'll tell her
part of the truth. That it didn't work out.'

He noticed her fingers: paper-pale, slender, and bare
of rings.

'It was never supposed to.'

He said the words. Felt them fall—guillotines through
the air. Hope severed. Completely.

'I'll get the car.'

She nodded.

Silence. Sometimes settled, sometimes awkward, sometimes easy. Before, with Danny, it had felt like two people quietly sharing the same air. This time—this silence
as they drove along the highway, past the familiar sights
that only a few days ago she had been desperate never

to see again—it was breathless…as if the air was too thin to share.

Gasping.

She longed to be home. Longed to breathe naturally again. Longed to see Babs and for this giant Dubai adventure to be over. She'd given it a go. She'd given up her settled little London life in which she'd been making a difference. She'd come out here, chasing her dream of husband and happiness. And if she'd felt whiplash from the wreckage of her time with Nick, it was nothing to what she was going to feel when *this* horrific crash was over.

Danny was the fast lane, the big time, the super-league. She'd allowed herself to get caught up in his world, but she wasn't cut out to be part of his set. She liked things small, manageable, quiet. Reliable. She wanted an easy life where love was warm and comforting, not hot and choking.

Fingers burned once? Whole body incinerated now.

'Have you told Babs you're on your way?'

Silence finally broken. His voice was strained—fingernails scraping a chalkboard.

She swallowed. 'Not yet.' She closed her eyes, pressing down on hot wet tears.

'I want there to be someone to meet you, Georgia.'

She thought of Friday night in the pub. She thought of wiping a cloth along the bar top, emptying the drip trays, chasing out the last of the customers. She thought of stacking chairs on top of tables, sweeping the floor, closing the large oak doors. She thought of sliding the bolts across, locking the world out and herself and Babs in. She thought of home. Longed for it.

'No, there's no need. Babs has the pub to run—there's

no way I'm going to get her out of her bed to wait for me at Heathrow. I'm perfectly capable of getting the bus.'

'The *bus*? You're not getting on a bus at seven in the morning with a truckload of designer luggage. Forget it.'

When was it going to stop?

'Okay. How about I get a helicopter home? Would that make you feel better? Have you stopped to think that no matter what I do from here on in it'll have nothing to do with you?'

She could see him squeeze the steering wheel a little tighter but she let her eyes rest there only a moment.

'I...I just care about you, Georgia.'

She hardly heard him. Whispered words.

'I know,' she whispered back.

He reached for her hand. She let him hold it. Let him squeeze it.

'I said I wanted us to stay friends.'

He took his eyes off the road and looked at her, and she traced the lines of his profile, imprinting them one last time.

'I meant it.'

She looked away. The night passed by outside. The hustle of Dubai—his home town.

'But we tried to keep it strictly business at the palace. And...' A half-smile played at his mouth. 'Well, that wasn't exactly successful, was it?'

'No, not exactly,' she said, thinking of awakening after her dream, the heat of his body, the fire of desire that had erupted between them—the flames that nothing would extinguish. 'Do you think it's possible? For us to keep in touch and not want to climb inside each other?'

They were already passing signs for the airport. That feeling of breathlessness was creeping over her again.

'No.'

'A clean break, then?'

'Yes.'

Suffocating, heavy, dense and dark—the air in the car as it rolled along the highway. Where she got the strength to hold back the emotion that battered at her she would never know. London faded. Babs faded. All she felt was the wrenching, heaving sense of being hauled away from her north star.

Hold on, she told herself. *Hold on—because it will get better, it will ease. And the world will right itself again. This time will pass. And you will be the better for it.*

He parked. He got a trolley. He put her cases on it. He moved with strength, with grace, with certainty. He cut a path—she walked at his side. She dropped her bags, checked her flight. LHR—the letters called her home.

He took her as far as he could. Cupped her cheek. She kissed his palm. Bright blue eyes…dark green gaze. No overflow of emotion.

She was going home.

He was Dubai.

CHAPTER TEN

THROWING ORDERS AROUND, throwing money around, throwing himself into work. All things that in the past had been guaranteed to deliver the numbing sense of satisfaction Danny craved. This time? It was taking a little longer.

Life had not so much rolled as rocketed along since the Friday night he'd driven Georgia to the airport to get the two a.m. flight home. He'd almost welcomed the searing pain that he'd known would follow, because it would remind him that other people always let you down—that if you could rely on anything in this world, it was that. The difference this time was that no matter how hard he tried he couldn't blame Georgia for anything other than bringing sunshine into his life.

So he'd created a punishing schedule of exercise and work, meetings and site visits. He'd managed the media for his project and the media for his personal life. He'd made a call back home, spoken personally to Mark, to his mother, and—when she'd finally crawled out of her self-imposed exile—his sister too. He'd looked at the world through Georgia's lens. It had been the next best thing to having her.

He'd fielded and shielded and brought this baby home. So he should be sitting back now, in the executive hospitality area that looked out over a football pitch—the first of the sports arenas to be completed—with absolute pride.

But he wasn't. He was switching a glass of warm champagne between one hand and another. He was shaking the hands and patting the backs of the next team in town, the company owners who would come here to wine and dine and entertain. He was mingling with international football players he might once have been impressed by. And he was avoiding the ubiquitous wives and girlfriends, and the female predators who were here with no other game on their minds than husband-bagging.

The news that his new wife was on another continent had quietened down, and so many months had now passed that speculation had moved on from *when* she would be back to *if* she would be back.

Of course, regardless of whether he was married, there was always a steady stream of women who would happily act as his personal hostess. The thought left him cold.

The Al-Jafar penthouse lay empty.

He still hadn't done anything about the divorce. He'd been far too busy. And it was surely better if the clean break they'd agreed upon included a communication blackout. Which included any communication from lawyers. Predictably, she had been in touch to start the ball rolling—but he had called time out…for now. Just until he passed another one of his project milestones. Like this one. The Dubai International Soccer Stadium.

He smiled and he laughed, he posed for photos and moved from group to group, feeling as empty as the cavernous arena they were all there to celebrate. One milestone passed—another seven to go. And that didn't include the milestones that were stacking up in his personal life.

He had to take the next step. And soon. He knew it made sense—because the other option didn't. He didn't do U-turns. They were a sign of weakness. And he didn't do long-term commitment. That was a sign of lunacy. And in those few wild moments he would admit to having, when he found himself dialling her number or checking flights to London, thank God common sense had prevailed. Misery too—but that would pass.

Life had been fine before Georgia and it would be fine again after. It was just another milestone away.

'You are the toast of the town, my friend.'

Sheikh Salim stood at his shoulder: quiet, modest in his pristine *dish-dasha*—the madding crowd's second favourite attraction.

'I think we should be proud of what we've done, Salim. I don't mind who knows it.'

The words came easily—he could say all the right things, could act appropriately. He could stand shoulder to shoulder with the man he'd spent years emulating and take the plaudits and the praise and the validation for being one of Dubai's brightest stars. But he couldn't recapture the buzz he'd used to feel.

He had more money than he knew what to do with. Should he buy more cars, a bigger house? Take a holiday? God no. He could think of nothing worse. The only things that killed the creeping, suffocating unease were work and exercise.

'Yes. Against the odds, we've done a good thing,' Salim went on. 'And we both know that your stance on wages and conditions has caught worldwide media interest and saved our town from another negative onslaught.'

'Your stance too—you're just more measured about how you say and do things. I still haven't learned the fine art of understatement.'

'Ah, you're very hard on yourself. You've learned a great many things, even in the time I've known you. But forgive me when I say there is one huge lesson that you don't yet want to learn. However, time will tell… time will tell.'

Danny turned sharply. It was not the first time his friend had made a statement like that and he knew perfectly well that he was referring to Georgia. He'd made no secret of his disappointment that they had dissolved their marriage after so little time. He asked after her frequently. And even though Danny rebuffed his questions every time he had a feeling that there was some other line of communication open.

'I am particularly proud of the opportunities we are now able to offer the families of our workforce,' Salim said, and nodded to himself.

Danny wasn't sure what else had been cooking in the background, but he knew that shrewdness and compassion were equally measured in this man. And with his own time so tight he'd left some of the softer sides of the project to those with the capacity. But now his antennae were tingling. Salim was looking almost smug.

'I haven't had a recent update from the charities board. Is there anything I should know? You know I don't like surprises.'

'No, you don't. But sometimes it's good to roll with the punches. And I think you'll particularly enjoy rolling with this one. Anyway, we'll give an update shortly,' he said, pointing at the podium, where PR and media people were now gathering. He nodded across the room. 'But first, if you don't mind, I think I see your brother. I would like to talk thoroughbreds for a moment, in amongst all this football, so if you'll excuse me…?'

Danny watched him. The room watched him.

Having the rest of Team Ryan here hadn't been *his* idea, but he'd seen the sense and he'd felt the glow of pride from his mother. And that, he supposed, was something. No, this bright idea was down to Salim, whose interest in Danny's personal life had taken a sharp turn for the worryingly intense.

Georgia looked down at her shoes. A bad choice. Her toes were pinched and the strap behind her ankle was already working up a blister. She'd forgotten how much her feet swelled up in the heat, and just walking to the stadium had taken her out of the coach's arctic air-con and into the midday inferno. But she loved these red shoes—loved the memory they brought back. And it was just a coincidence that they set off her Portobello Market power dress perfectly.

She looked around at her little crew. Their wide-eyed wonder had been replaced with nervous smiles as they stared through the glass doors at the array of world-class football players—their heroes. So far she had avoided staring at anything other than her notes, but she knew he was in there. She could feel him. She just wished she could be as confident as Sheikh Salim that Danny would be happy about her involvement in this aspect of the charity. She wished she'd had a chance to brief him personally before now, but it wasn't to be. She could only assume someone else had done it.

Her stomach pirouetted again. It had been twelve whole months since she had seen him. Six months of them were dust. Gone. She had been in a walking coma. Learning how to breathe, how to live, how to smile. How to look at a sunset or walk in the park or ride in a car without thinking of him.

Babs had stood sentry better than the Queen's Guard.

She'd asked no questions but had listened faithfully when Georgia had finally been able to form sentences. She'd wept and hugged and adored her when she'd told her she had brought home enough money to clear her debts and buy back the pub. The only time she'd raised an eyebrow and made her feelings known had been when Georgia had told her she was heading back to Dubai.

'You know how hard I've been working on this twinning programme,' she'd told her sister. 'You know that the apprentice soccer coaches here will never get a chance like it again. To train the children of the immigrant workers in the very stadium they've been building! To meet football legends!'

Of course Babs did know. She'd been there every step of the way with her. She'd been instrumental in convincing her, after Salim's wife had been in touch, that it would be the very thing to get her out of her dank little prison. And Georgia knew that it was only concern for her battered heart that had had Babs wincing and wringing her hands when she'd told her about the trip.

But that was then. And this was now.

Three months to plan and execute. To prep her teenaged coaches, get them passports, arrange accommodation and ensure they knew the ground rules of this opportunity of a lifetime. And here they were—ready to rub shoulders with their heroes, ready to tell the UAE press about this philanthropic act from United Arab Leisure—also known as Danny Ryan and Sheikh Salim al Baraka.

And she could do this. She could pass this test. There were more important things than her wounded pride, her broken heart.

He'd never called her. Not once. The only contact had

been a missive from his lawyer asking to delay their divorce—she supposed for some tax or corporate reason.

She had slowly blown out every candle of hope, one by one. And then she'd sat in a dark, dank pool of despair until finally she'd realised he was never coming for her. And then slowly, slowly, she'd put herself back together again.

The only problem was the paint wasn't dry.

The door opened.

'Ready for you now.'

She squared her shoulders, gave each of her boys and girls a bracing hug and a winning smile, then led them through.

Panoramic views of the stadium…up close and personal views of the world's most elite football players… the flash and clatter of cameras lighting their path.

They took their places.

Mrs Georgia Ryan read her nameplate. She sat behind it, unperturbed.

Danny watched. His hand went to his jaw. He should have known. Should have realised. Should feel angry at being duped. But he could only feel awe.

Georgia Anne Ryan. Even more beautiful than before. Even more composed. Drawing every eye. A goddess.

She hadn't seen him. He was way at the back of the space but he was moving to her, slowly weaving his way in and out of the glitzy and the glamorous, as if she was pulling him in on some golden thread.

Salim caught his eye, held it for a moment, then looked away, satisfied.

She sat on the podium with six kids. They looked at her as she spoke, as she radiated her charm. She was more brightly illuminated than the flashes from ten rows of snappers and hacks. She told the room—the world—about her work. And he felt even more awed. All about her? Nothing was *ever* all about her. It was always all about everyone else.

She told of her charity work for United Arab Leisure. She told of working with inner-city London kids, keeping them in the system through sport and encouraging them to pay back through becoming coaches themselves. She spoke of the shock of the English kids when they'd learned that even in their poverty they had so much more than the children of immigrant workers in Dubai. She spoke of the fortunate children of diplomats and industrialists. Of how all of them shared the same thing—the need to be loved. The universal leveller.

She spoke of her inspirational visit to Sheikh Salim's palace, of meeting his family and witnessing how wealth there did not mean affluence or arrogance. It meant respect and responsibility. She spoke and this collection of the talented, the smart, the beautiful and the rich all halted their chatter. They *listened*.

'Georgia, this is your first trip back to Dubai in a year, is it not? Speculation has been rife that you've moved home—that your marriage is over. Can we assume that your appearance here suggests otherwise?'

He saw faces turn to him. Then to her. He watched her absorb the question, saw a shadow roll over her eyes. She looked down at the desk. The air stilled. Became charged, tense, taut. She was going to lose her nerve.

He felt the flare of anger—so unfamiliar in him now.

He saw faces. His mother, his sister, his brother. Sheikh Salim. He could almost feel them willing him to be calm. Of course he would be calm. He wouldn't let anyone down. Never again. Eleven years in this town had taught him well. He had gained so much—wisdom, money, power—but the one thing he hadn't managed to gain was peace. Not since the moment he'd said goodbye to that intoxicating redhead. And he had to let her know.

But when his eyes found her through the glare of lights and people he saw strength. She sat like a queen, utterly, resolutely, undeniably regal. She was smiling. Commanding. Inspiring.

'Home is just a four-letter word. It's not about geography. It's about love.'

She told the room. She told him.

There was complete silence. And then the cameras started clattering and flashing. She spoke through the white noise.

'My marriage—your marriage—any marriage—is worthless without love. Love is the most important thing for any of us. For these young people from London…for the children who've made new homes here in Dubai, joining their mothers and fathers working in this wonderful city. It doesn't matter how much money flows, how many cars or jewels or houses you have. Home is love and love is where you make your home.'

The room erupted into applause and questions and photographs. Whistles from his boys—a cheer from Tommy. Georgia and her team stood up. She was beaming, but he knew her. She was shaken too.

He moved to her. Nothing on this earth could stop him.

She was shepherding her teenagers through the double doors when he caught her. Placed his hand on her shoulder. The bone, the supple muscle, the soft skein of auburn hair brushed his hand. The sweet joy of touching her again… She spun round. Her beautiful face… Her understanding eyes…

Her loving smile suddenly faltered. 'Danny!'

'Georgia.'

'It's lovely to see you.'

'We need to talk.'

'Oh, okay. I assumed you'd been briefed? I hope it was all explained well in advance? I got a bit worried when you hadn't been in touch. Are you happy with it? Do you like what we've done?'

'I… Yes, of course. It's wonderful work. Georgia, you look… I've missed you.'

She took a moment to follow. 'Thanks. I tried to look my best. You know me and my market stall finds.'

'I missed you. I still miss you.'

Round about them was buzz and blur. People moving…the party starting. Chatter made louder by alcohol and brand-new gossip.

He wanted to shield her and protect her, but she didn't need him to do that. She had proved she was strong and true and moral. She had proved that she was kind and generous and caring. She wasn't the type of woman who made a promise and walked away. She was utterly, completely, resolutely loyal.

She was trust.

'I missed you too.'

But she looked askance—she was unsure of him. He had to prove himself to her. And that meant taking it slow, taking it at her pace—not his. *He* didn't care that they were in the middle of a press frenzy in a country with strict laws about public displays of affection. As far as he was concerned he wanted to stake his claim on her right here, right now, and anyone who didn't want to see could look away.

But he'd come a long way since the last time he'd seen her. He didn't growl at people when they didn't do things his way. He'd learned patience and tolerance. And he had her to thank. Her to tell.

'Are your kids all right without you for a while? Can we go somewhere to talk?'

She still looked unsure.

'Five minutes, Georgia. That's all I ask.'

She turned that face up to his and he had to hold his hands at his sides. With every fibre of his body he held himself in check.

'Of course.'

She followed him through the forest of people. Followed his strong, broad back and felt herself slipping into a dream.

He turned round every couple of seconds to make sure she was right behind him. And that image—the cast of his cheekbones, the arch of his brow, the question in his eyes—it was the same image she'd seen for twelve months whenever she closed her eyes.

He led them out of the terraced space and down a flight of wide, pristine stairs. The wall of noise and chatter faded and then, as they exited onto another tier through more double doors, disappeared. She tried to keep up with him, but her shoes were not the best for tripping down flights of stairs.

He stopped at the bottom of the next flight. Waited until she'd reached him. Held his hand out for her.

A gesture of peace, she supposed. She slipped her fingers inside his. Warm and strong and tempting—but only a gesture. Whatever he had to say, she must remember how easily the world fell into place for him. She must be on her guard.

Then the crush of noise bore down on them again as the doors were opened. People were coming downstairs behind them, their happy chatter echoing.

'Let's find somewhere quiet.'

She went with him down another six flights. Heels clicking and heart pounding. Noise always above them. Finally they reached the ground. He checked each way, shook his head.

'Nothing else for it.'

His fingers still held hers tightly, purposefully.

'Have you been out on the pitch?'

Her eyes widened as she looked at where they were headed. To the football pitch itself. He led her out. Doors opened into a furnace of heat, a blaze of green grass. Vast tiers of empty seats in primary colours flanked the sides. A huge canopied glass roof, half open, shielded the ground. It was immense and humbling.

He led her to the dugout. That was far enough.

She halted. 'Danny. I can't be away from the kids for too long. What is it that you want to say?'

He sat down, urged her to sit next to him. He shook his head. Swallowed. 'I don't know where to begin.'

She looked at him—this man who'd rocked her world. The suit was as sharp, the hair slightly shorter, stubble slightly thicker, but everything else was exactly the same—the blindingly handsome features, the intense, demanding eyes. Memories sharpened within her, seducing her with their sweetness. How easy it would be to succumb.

'I've run this through in my head so many times.' He half laughed. 'You'd think I'd be word-perfect.'

She felt the flicker of something—recognition? Had he been suffering as she had? Even so... She crossed her arms and sat back. She would listen, but she wouldn't cede. She couldn't.

'I wanted to get in touch.'

'So what stopped you?'

He looked past her for a moment. 'I honestly don't

know. I suppose I thought I'd get back the equilibrium I had before I met you. I thought it was bound to return soon.'

He stared at her. Took two strong hands and tugged her arms free from their wrap around her body. Held her hands. Rubbed his fingers over hers.

'It hasn't. It won't.'

She closed her eyes, battling the urge to melt into him, forgive him.

'Georgia. I've been more miserable this past year than at any other point in my life—even after putting Mark in hospital. I've thought about you every day—every moment of every day to begin with. I couldn't bear it that I couldn't reach out and touch you, see your smile or hear your voice.'

He lifted her hand closer, held it between them as if it was a chalice, put his mouth to her fingers, dusted them with kisses.

'But if I've learned one thing it's that it's not always all about me. You taught me that. And I couldn't be sure that getting in touch would be the right thing for you...or me.'

She swallowed. He was so, *so* hard to resist. The universe would always fall into order for him. But she couldn't go through the misery of the past year again.

'Seeing you today—everything suddenly makes sense. I have to have you in my life—I can't let you leave me again. I'll do whatever it takes.'

Right into her eyes he trained his pure blue gaze. Right into the heart of her. And it felt as if the giant scars on her heart were beginning to heal just with that look. But the scars were deep. It would take more than hope to mend her fully.

'I don't know if you can do whatever it takes, Danny. I don't know what that would be.'

He tugged her hand to his chest, leaned into her. More of him stole over her—his scent, his energy, his absolute will to get whatever he wanted.

'You. Me. Together. That's all we need—we can work out the rest.'

She shook her head. 'I can't just be another project for you to manage. And I absolutely *won't* be an object for you to vent your emotions on.'

'I know, Georgia. That's why I'm sure that you're the one for me. You inspire me—you challenge me. You see that the world is made up of people—not stuff. You make me a much, much better person. And I want—I *need* to prove that to you.'

He stared at her with such intensity. Opened his mouth. Closed it again. He lifted his hands to cup the sides of her face. His eyes blazed. He swallowed.

'I love you.'

As if all the pain, the hurt, the agony had simply melted she felt her face break into a smile, and the words she'd held in her mouth since she'd met him poured out.

'I love you too.'

She reached for him where he sat rigidly, waiting for her pardon. She touched his face. His eyes begged her forgiveness. She smiled at him to grant it.

'I'll show you every day of my life. I want to make you as happy as you make me. Anything and everything I need to do for you—for us—I swear I'll do it.'

He grabbed her then. Stood her up. Used his hands to trace the memories of his love for her. Her hair, her face, her shoulders, her waist. He grabbed her close and rocked her. Tilted her back and claimed the mouth he'd spent twelve months imagining he could live without. He tasted her strength and goodness. He drank of her serenity and her grace. He would never, ever get enough.

'Marry me.'

She smiled and laughed against his mouth. 'Again?'

He lifted her off her heels and spun her in slow, loving circles.

'Again. Properly. Call Babs—call her now—get her to fly over. My family are already here.'

'They're here?' She slid down his body. 'Seriously?'

He took another kiss.

'Seriously. Salim's idea. It's all good. I've been over to Ireland a few times and it was time to bring my mum here.'

'Was she up there? When I was speaking?'

He nodded. 'Oh, yes. They all were.'

'Even your brother?'

He nodded his head. 'Yes, all of them. It's a long story...for another time.' He traced her lips with his thumb, trailed it down her pale throat, laid it on her chest. Closed his eyes and savoured her. 'Georgia, we need to get married. You need to be my bride properly. We need to make plans.'

'You're still planning?'

'Definitely. One plan—that involves you. And me. And the rest of our lives. Wherever you want to spend it.'

'Seriously? You'd live anywhere? But you're in the middle of this with Salim. It's your biggest deal ever. You could never walk away from this.'

He shrugged slightly. 'I would for you. If I've learned anything—and trust me when I say I've been a model pupil this past year—it's that all this...' he swung his arm round the vast arena, the immaculate grass, the row upon row of seats, including in them the restaurants and shops and other arenas which were about to make him richer than Croesus '...is worthless without you.'

She smiled her larger-than-life smile and wrapped her sweeter-than-heaven body around him.

'Somehow I can't imagine you being a model pupil in anyone's class. And there's more here for me to do too—now that I know that Babs is settled I can get stuck into the charity work.'

'And I'm not blasting you—forcing you into a box or in any way coercing you to do anything other than what you want to do?'

She shook her head, smiled her largest smile. 'No way. I wouldn't let you. You know that.'

'I do. Let's tell the world, then.'

'Another press call?'

'I suppose we could thank them for forcing our first wedding. Let them know we're going to have a second.'

He walked her out onto the grass and there, in the centre circle, he dropped to his knee. He held out his arms and pulled her down. Kissed her hand, kissed her mouth.

And above them a wall of catcalls and applause and blinding white flashes lit up their moment and honoured their love.

* * * * *

MILLS & BOON®

Want to get more from Mills & Boon?

Here's what's available to you if you join the exclusive **Mills & Boon eBook Club** today:

✦ *Convenience – choose your books each month*
✦ *Exclusive – receive your books a month before anywhere else*
✦ *Flexibility – change your subscription at any time*
✦ *Variety – gain access to eBook-only series*
✦ *Value – subscriptions from just £1.99 a month*

So visit **www.millsandboon.co.uk/esubs** today to be a part of this exclusive eBook Club!

EBOOK_SUBS_2014

MILLS & BOON®

Why shop at millsandboon.co.uk?

Each year, thousands of romance readers find their perfect read at millsandboon.co.uk. That's because we're passionate about bringing you the very best romantic fiction. Here are some of the advantages of shopping at www.millsandboon.co.uk:

* **Get new books first**—you'll be able to buy your favourite books one month before they hit the shops

* **Get exclusive discounts**—you'll also be able to buy our specially created monthly collections, with up to 50% off the RRP

* **Find your favourite authors**—latest news, interviews and new releases for all your favourite authors and series on our website, plus ideas for what to try next

* **Join in**—once you've bought your favourite books, don't forget to register with us to rate, review and join in the discussions

Visit **www.millsandboon.co.uk**
for all this and more today!

MILLS_WEB